NATURALLY, AXEL WANTED THE BEST PAD IN L.A.

He drove past a mansion that had work crews swarming all over it. Abruptly he did a U-turn and pulled into the driveway. He walked up the steps, his eyes on the workmen.

"I'm Axel Foley, City of Beverly Hills, building inspection. You look like the foreman. I bet you can read."

"For years now."

"Right angles! Right angles! Wait till the owners find out!"

"They're in Hawaii for a week, but what the hell . . ."

"Right angles! This is a major screw-up. You could all get fired!"

"Wait a minute," the foreman said. "This place would be round as a doughnut without . . ."

Axel addressed all the workmen now. "You'll get your paycheck at the end of the week."

The workmen looked at Axel. Slowly they began packing up their tools and straggled down the driveway.

Axel stood on the lawn until they were all out of sight. Then he got his suitcase from the car. When he pushed the front door open, he walked through a tiled entrance hall as big as his whole apartment in Detroit.

Axel dropped his bag.

BEVERLY HILLS

Cop II

a novel by Robert Tine

based on a screenplay
written by Larry Ferguson
and Warren Skaaren

story by
Eddie Murphy & Robert D. Wachs

based on characters created by
Danilo Bach and Daniel Petrie, Jr.

PUBLISHED BY POCKET BOOKS NEW YORK

This novel is a work of fiction. Names, characters, places and incidents are either the product of the author's imagination or are used fictitiously. Any resemblance to actual events or locales or persons, living or dead, is entirely coincidental.

Another *Original* publication of POCKET BOOKS

POCKET BOOKS, a division of Simon & Schuster, Inc.
1230 Avenue of the Americas, New York, N.Y. 10020

ISBN: 0-671-64521-8

First Pocket Books printing May 1987

10 9 8 7 6 5 4 3 2 1

POCKET and colophon are registered trademarks of Simon & Schuster, Inc.

BEVERLY HILLS COP is a trademark of Paramount Pictures Corporation.

Printed in the U.S.A.

BEVERLY HILLS

Cop II

CHAPTER
ONE

Axel Foley, the pride of the Detroit Police Department, was getting dressed for work. Normally, this would not have been an event of any great importance, either to Axel or the world at large: blue jeans, Mumford High sweatshirt, running shoes, and it was done. But Axel's clothes were different now. They had names.

He whipped open the sagging door of his beat-up closet and reached in, pulling out a crisp Karl Lagerfeld shirt. As he slipped into it, the adding machine in his head started working: one shirt, $250. The scratched top drawer of his battered dresser yielded a pair of hand-knit, silk Christian Dior socks: one pair socks, $75.

Axel slipped into his Nino Cerrutti suit. He stepped over to his dresser and checked himself in the mirror. He liked what he saw and flashed himself a grin. One suit, $2,000. A life of crime certainly did wonders for your wardrobe. It was a shame, he thought, that none of this stuff belonged to him. It was all the property of the Detroit Police Department. If you were supposed to be a rich criminal—or an undercover cop impersonating a rich criminal—you couldn't dress out of the Sears catalog. You had to look boss; you had to look the part. Axel looked the part.

He expertly knotted his silk Jacard tie ($300) and slipped a wafer-thin Patek Philip watch ($5,000) onto his wrist. He stepped back to the dresser, slipped his Browning 9mm into the police-issue holster ($6.95) in the small of his back and wondered when Giorgio Armani was going to come out with a designer gun. He looked approvingly at all $7,625 of himself and grinned again.

"I'd fuck me," he said aloud. "But would I respect myself in the morning?" He cracked a huge smile at his image in the mirror.

But Axel's transformation wasn't quite complete. His blue Chevy Nova, the one with the cracked white vinyl roof and more dents than a bumper car, had been temporarily retired for this case. In its place Axel had chosen something a little more up-market. It was a fire-engine red, Testa Rossa Ferrari. It was a lot better looking than his Chevy. And it went a *lot* faster.

Axel started the car in the garage of his building, slid the stickshift into first, and blasted off onto the Detroit streets. He rocketed down East Grand, the bright red car the only spot of color between the leaden Detroit River on his right and the broken-down, falling-in houses on his left. Kids playing in the spray of an open fire hydrant stopped to watch him pass. These were Detroit kids —street kids—and they were wise beyond their years.

"How much blow you think he moved to pay for that car?" asked an eight-year-old.

"Three keys downtown," said his ten-year-old

companion, "two if it was in Grosse Point or Bloom-
ington."

When Axel pulled up to the gate at the Detroit
Police Department garage, Bennie, the grizzled
guard, looked at him and shook his head in disgust.

Silently, the window of the Ferrari slid down and
Axel flashed Bennie his grin. "What's the matter,
Bennie? Never seen a rich black man before? Just
because my investments paid off doesn't mean I'm
not the same old Axel. You know, you should talk to
my broker, maybe he can get you into some good
things. . . ."

Bennie flipped up the gate pole. "Get outta here,
Foley."

Axel gunned the Ferrari into the gloomy garage
and parked. As he slid out of the supple leather seat,
he tapped the car lightly, affectionately. He thought
maybe he would ask the car to marry him. . . .

The detectives' squad room on the third floor was
just about as nice as the garage Axel had just left.
Detectives sat at broken-down desks pounding at the
bent keys of old manual typewriters. Here and there
suspects were handcuffed to dented gunmetal-gray
chairs, looking a little bored with a booking process
that a number of them had no doubt experienced
before. The tall windows of the room were covered
in a thick layer of soot—it looked like there was a
gray blizzard going on outside.

Axel strode past his brother police officers, all of
whom looked up as he passed.

"Hey, Foley," shouted Granby, an old cop with a

big belly that strained against his polyester shirt, "we only let *real* cops in here."

Axel never broke stride, he just grinned at Granby as he passed. "You still alive, Granby? I didn't notice till now."

"Very funny, Axel."

Orvis, a younger cop, came swooping down on Axel, his hands out in front of him like tentacles.

"Hey, Foley, can I touch you? I never touched anything that cost more than two hundred dollars before."

"Keep your sweaty hands off Nino," Axel commanded.

"Nino?" said Orvis. "Who the fuck is Nino? You call yourself Nino now?"

"The suit. That's its name. Nino."

"Can I touch it? I told you I never touched anything that cost—"

"What about your mother, Orvis? I heard she cost three bills."

Orvis's face fell. "Hey, man, no mother jokes."

Jeers filled the room. One of the suspects would have clapped if his hands hadn't been cuffed.

It was early in the morning in California and Andrew Bogomil, *genuinely* the pride of the Beverly Hills Police Department, jogged sure and steady along Ridgetop Road. His route took him deep into the hills of Beverly Hills. He passed the last of the estates of millionaires who slept soundly behind walls and strong gates, secure in the knowledge that a couple of hundred thousand dollars of security equipment ensured that their slumbers would not be disturbed.

Bogomil left the paved road and ran into the mist that hid a one-lane dirt track. It always surprised him that up here in the hills there was so much open land. Running way down the hills all the whole distance to the Pacific Ocean miles away, there were millions of people, all jammed in next to, or on top of, one another. Yet up here in the hills, horses still grazed. He could hear one whinnying off ahead of him in the mist.

He slowed his pace slightly and wiped the sweat from his brow using the bottom of his T-shirt as a towel. "Beverly Hills Police Department" was prominently stenciled across the chest. The mist lifted a little and Bogomil scanned the open ground ahead of him. It was an odd sight. Not far off was a large, round oil storage tank. He knew that oil was still pumped in Beverly Hills—oil, not movies, had been the cornerstone of the community's great wealth—but as far as Bogomil knew, any oil that was pumped was piped out of town as soon as it came out of the ground. So why a storage tank? He jogged over to it and ran around it, lightly brushing the steel plates with his hands as if to assure himself that the tank was real.

Then he ran on, although now he seemed less interested in his running than in a thought that was running through his mind.

Bogomil came to an abrupt halt and looked down at his feet. A single set of car tracks were set deep in the red, clayey mud. He looked down the track, following the tire trail with his eyes. He noticed that a few hundred yards on the car had turned around. He stood stock still for a moment, lost in thought.

The mist was lifting now and spread out below him he could see the city of Los Angeles, a huge patchwork quilt of roads, freeways, and houses stretching away for miles. But the sights on the desolate neighboring hillside interested him far more than the breathtaking view of the city. On the hillside a small herd of horses grazed, heads down to the grass, cropping mouthfuls with strong teeth. They moved easily and unafraid among the rhythmic up and down of the oil pumps that dotted the slope.

There were the oil pumps, he thought. . . . He turned around and looked at the lone storage tank. He started jogging back the way he had come. *Oil from the ground goes into the oil tank,* he thought. *Makes perfect sense.*

He ran a hundred yards or so, his Nikes slipping deep into the red mud. So why did this perfect sense . . . not add up?

As Bogomil returned to the paved road, a lone figure stood up from behind an outcropping of rock. He had been watching Bogomil since he ran onto the property, taking particular interest in his run around the oil tank. And he had read the words printed on Bogomil's T-shirt.

"Beverly Hills cop," the man said aloud. He spoke the words with distaste.

An hour later, Andrew Bogomil sat at his desk in the den of his home. He was freshly showered, shaved, and dressed for work, but he didn't feel the exhilaration that he usually felt after a good long run. The business section of the *Los Angeles Times* was spread open on his desk and he scrutinized it intently.

He hardly looked up when his daughter Jan came into the room carrying a cup of freshly brewed coffee for him. She was a year or two past twenty and lean, like her father. She was also pretty, her brown-blond hair falling gracefully to her shoulders. And she had inherited the same blue eyes that stared so intently at the newspaper.

Jan placed the coffee cup on the desk.

"Thanks hon," said Bogomil, his eyes still riveted to the newspaper.

Jan smiled to herself. That was her father: his power of concentration was astonishing. An earthquake could start at that moment and he wouldn't look up until he had finished and digested what he was reading.

"Dad," she said, speaking more or less to the top of his head, "I've got to work late tonight. Can you take care of yourself for dinner?"

Her father nodded without looking up. "Uh-huh."

She leaned over and kissed him on the cheek. "Bye, Dad."

"Bye," he said.

She was at the door when he finally raised his eyes from the paper. "Hey," he said, smiling broadly, "come back here. Call that a good-bye?" She walked back to her dear old dad and he gave her a kiss and hug. "Bye, honey. Drive safely."

"Don't I always?" she said, walking out the door.

"No," said Bogomil, "you don't."

He sat back in his chair and opened a drawer, taking out his shoulder holster and his gun. He carefully checked that there was no round in the chamber and that the safety was on before strapping on the holster. The .38 was snug under his arm. He picked up the phone and dialed a long-distance number. While he waited for his call to be answered, he carefully tore the business article he had been so interested in out of the paper and slipped it into a red folder. There were other papers in there too, and he was about to look them over for the hundredth time when his call was picked up at the other end.

"Detroit Police Department."

"Detective Axel Foley, please."

There was a moment's silence while the switchboard routed the call to Axel. Foley answered the phone on the first ring, but before Bogomil could say anything, Axel was off and running. "You have reached the White House. The First Lady and I are out taking money from the poor and giving it to our powerful friends. . . ."

Bogomil smiled and tried to say something. But he was too slow. Axel had beaten him to the punch again.

"So if you have any solutions to unsolvable world problems like the Middle East, Russia—or know whatever happened to Michael Jackson—leave a message." Axel's voice dropped an octave and shifted from white to black. "Otherwise, don't be botherin' me."

"Axel," Bogomil said finally, "it's Bogomil."

Axel was visibly delighted to hear the older man's

voice. He leaned back in his chair. "Andrew! How's it goin'? Are you police chief yet?"

Bogomil frowned. No, he wasn't police chief yet. It looked like he was never going to make chief. But he kept his voice light. "No, Axel, not yet. Have you made commander yet?"

"Nah," said Axel, "but I'm almost there. I'm on my last undercover and I miss it already."

"Miss it? How come?"

Axel looked down at his splendid clothes. *Well, for one thing, you got to dress a lot better on undercover.* But it was more than that. If he was going up the chain of command, that meant less action. "You know how it is, Andrew, now I'll have to sit around in meetings with jerks like me. Shit, I'll probably end up like you. Soft belly, corrupt . . ."

Bogomil smiled, but he didn't have a comeback. Instead he got down to business. "Listen, Axel, I'm going to have to cancel out on our fishing trip."

Axel felt a twinge of disappointment—the trip had been planned for months. "Well, shit . . . I was going to teach you how to rough up a five-hundred-pound marlin."

"Sorry, Axel."

"No, but I'm glad really," he said, "I'm up to my ass in undercover on some credit-card fakes. I'm real close to zooming the bastards." He paused. "But what's with you? Beverly Hills got a big push on to wipe out jaywalking and other crimes against neatness?"

Bogomil laughed, but put a protective hand on the folder. *That* was what he was going to be working on. "Yeah, some fiend has been kidnapping all the private workout instructors. People are losing muscle tone. There's panic in the streets."

"That's ugly," said Axel, mock-serious, "very ugly. If you don't mind, I'll take Detroit any day of the week."

"It's all yours, Axel."

"No, but really man, what's so important that you can't take a week off for some fishing?"

Bogomil paused. He wasn't keeping anything from Axel, it was just that he wasn't sure what he had . . . yet. "It's . . . I'm not sure what it is really. I'll fill you in when I get it straight myself." Bogomil glanced at his wristwatch. "Look, Axel, I'm late. I have to go. You take care of yourself, okay?"

"Hey, don't worry about me. I'm a new man. I'm going to be a commander, a leader of men, I got to look straight, think straight, *be* straight. Hey, punch Rosewood in the eye for me, will you?"

Bogomil shook his head and smiled. "Bye, Axel. I'll call you in a week."

Axel hung up and thought about the call for a moment. It didn't surprise him all that much. Andrew Bogomil was a good cop. Duty first—fun later. Axel had a different philosophy—the duty was the fun.

CHAPTER TWO

Rodeo Drive, Beverly Hills. The richest street in the richest community in the world. Axel's Ferrari wouldn't turn a head here. By midmorning there were already five Testa Rossas parked on Rodeo and three more over on Wilshire. There were more Rolls Royces jockeying for parking spaces than there were pedestrians on the sidewalk. Big stretch limos, their windows tinted black to protect the rich and famous passengers from gawking tourists, plied up and down the streets of the main shopping district like yachts.

The residents of Beverly Hills would have thought that Axel's Nino Cerrutti suit was a nice piece of clothing. Just the thing to wear to lunch at Spago or the Bistro Gardens—but hey, no big deal, really; there were suits as good and as expensive to be had on every block. Big money in Detroit was small change here.

And of all the exclusive, expensive shops in Beverly Hills, none was quite as exclusive or expensive as Adriano's. Anywhere else on earth, shopping was relatively simple. You put your money in your pocket, went into a store, and bought what you wanted—or could afford. But not in Beverly Hills, and certainly not at Adriano's.

At Adriano's you had to call first to make an appointment to shop. But it wasn't that simple. Only after Adriano's had decided that you were the right kind of person, the type of person Adriano's wanted to sell to, might they—maybe—give you an appointment. And if, heaven forbid, you should show up *without* an appointment, then Raul, the handsome, but burly and well-muscled keeper of the door, would see you quietly but politely and firmly on your way.

Raul ran his eye over the black Cadillac limo that pulled up to the curb in front of him. He sniffed. He had seen the wrong kind of people get out of the right kind of car before. The chauffeur scurried around to the passenger door and opened it. Raul watched.

First one beautiful leg appeared, sheathed in a perfect black silk stocking. Then another. Even Raul's attention was piqued—he couldn't wait to see the rest. And when Karla Fry slipped out of the car and stood, all six sexy feet of her, on the sidewalk in front of him, he knew instantly that she was just the kind of person Adriano's gave an appointment to. Hell, if it was up to him, he'd open the store Christmas Day for this one.

Raul looked her up and down and then took the tour again. Her black hair cascaded to her shoulders. Perfect breasts—he just knew they were—heaved under a silk blouse. She was smiling, a smile that seemed to radiate heat at him. He felt as if he were getting a tan just standing in front of her.

But he couldn't see her eyes. She wore those reflecting sunglasses. All he could see as he stared at her was himself staring at her. But he could imagine those eyes, dark and smoky and . . .

She had dropped her purse. It fell to the sidewalk and snapped open, scattering a comb, a compact, a wallet, some loose change. Instantly Raul was on his knees picking up the odds and ends and trying to think of some dynamite line that would make her, this million-dollar apparition, fall in love with him, a doorman.

But she did all the talking and she did it from behind the snout of a snub-nosed, nickel-plated .38. That definitely caught Raul's eye.

"Do as I say, honey," she murmured as if talking to her lover. "Understand?"

Raul nodded. It was his policy to do anything for anyone who had a gun pointed at him.

A smile flitted across her perfect features. "Good boy. Stand up slowly, walk ahead of me, and open the door. I'll *try* to be gentle."

Raul stood up slowly, just the way she told him to. He wasn't the brightest guy in the world, but it struck him now that Adriano's was about to be taken down, robbed, by the sexiest woman he had ever seen.

"The key," she said softly. "Unlock the door."

He pulled the key out of his uniform pocket and unlocked the stately portals of Adriano's. The door swung open and Raul, followed by the former love of his life, stepped inside.

Adriano's was a cool, silent, chrome-and-glass cathedral dedicated to selling the finest, rarest jewelry, furs, and clothing in the world. The air smelled of money. Not a sound from the street entered this ostentatious temple. A few women strolled from display case to display case while an Adriano's salesperson hovered nearby ready to do the bidding of the very rich who had been deemed fit to spend their money there. On the mezzanine level was the jewelry section, the rare and precious gems catching the light from the enormous crystal chandelier that hung from the vaulted ceiling.

Nancy, the hostess who checked appointments, was seated behind a sleek, uncluttered desk just inside the front door. She looked up and saw Raul and the woman behind him. She certainly looked like Adriano's material. She looked down at her appointment book to see who was scheduled for 11:30. No one. She looked up again, and this time she noticed that there was the barrel of a gun laid against Raul's ear.

"Hey," was all that Nancy could think to say.

Karla whispered to Raul: "Lock the door and step away from it, baby." Her voice was as smooth as satin.

Nancy stood up. "What are you—" Adriano—whose real name was Adrian Applethorpe—was going to kill her when he heard about this.

"Shut up," spat Karla. "Lock the door," she cooed in Raul's ear. Raul did an almost military about-face and with trembling hands locked the door.

Nancy felt real fear now. There was something in the woman's voice that told her that she would not hesitate to use that lethal-looking little gun if she chose to. Adriano's had some nice stuff, but it wasn't worth getting shot over. In an instant, Nancy decided she was going to do what she was told, live through this, and find another job. In Iowa.

The little drama unfolding at the reception desk had caught the attention of the few shoppers and their sales assistants. They had all stopped to stare at Karla.

One woman, who might as well have had her bank balance written on her Valentino suit, observed: "She's got a gun."

Antoine, up until that moment her favorite salesperson—so charming, so attentive, so French—lost his accent. "No shit," he said in a voice that sounded more Peoria than Paris.

"Okay," Karla shouted, not purring now, "all of you on the floor." No one moved. "Do it!" she ordered. Some of them whimpering slightly, the shoppers lay down on the thick, plush carpet, most of them trying to remember what it was the police said they were supposed to do when things like this happened. Antoine remembered first. *No heroics.* The police always said that you shouldn't try to be a hero. *No heroics,* he said over and over to himself, as if it were his mantra.

From the mezzanine level came a voice. A very annoyed voice. Francesco, one of the floor managers, looked over the ornate gold railing to the amazing little scene below.

"What," he whined, "do you think you are doing?"

Karla raised the gun and aimed it directly at Francesco. "Get your ass down here," she said by way of explanation.

"I will like hell."

No heroics, Antoine chanted to himself.

The single shot seemed to rock the building to its

foundations. A huge chunk of the gold banister an inch or two from Francesco's perfectly manicured hands exploded. Through the acrid smoke, Karla spoke again.

"Move."

Francesco had changed his mind. He stumbled down the stairs hoping that he too would be allowed to lie down on the nice soft carpet. But Karla, who strode to meet him at the bottom of the steps, had other plans for him. She grabbed a handful of his cashmere sweater, hustled him across the selling floor, and pushed him into a hallway at the back of the store. There was the large steel service entrance, the back door to Adriano's.

She nudged the back of his neck with the little pistol.

"Open it."

He fumbled with his keys for a moment, very conscious of the gun barrel, still warm from the single shot, pushed in at the base of his skull. Despite this, he succeeded in opening the door.

He didn't think he could be any more frightened than he was already, but on opening the door his fear doubled. Standing there, blocking the entire doorway, were two men dressed in black from head to toe. Both had stockings pulled down over their faces, distorting their features, making them look monstrous. One of them wore a shoulder holster holding the largest gun Francesco had ever seen. The man looked like he had a refrigerator under his armpit.

"Jesus, Mary," Francesco said. But that was all he said. He had done his part. Karla stepped forward and delivered a short, sharp punch to Francesco's jaw. His eyes closed and he slid down the wall, his legs turning to rubber beneath him. He was out cold and never had the chance to consider who he could sue for all this.

A van reversed up the alley, stopping with a screech of tires at Adriano's rear door. The driver swung out of the seat and threw open the double doors of the truck. He began to haul a ramp out of the back and gave a thumbs-up sign to Karla. She nodded, gestured to the two guys in masks, and the three of them ran back into the store. Everyone was still on the floor. No one had been a hero.

Legs spread wide, Karla stood over Raul and Nancy, the gun in her right hand aimed at Raul's head. In her left hand she held a stopwatch. She tapped the button and set the clock ticking.

"Two minutes!" she yelled.

Like sprinters at the starting gun, the two masked men shot off, heading for their assigned positions. They had gone over the details a thousand times. Karla had told them again and again—nothing but furs and jewels. Leave the other stuff—the clothing, the leather. Furs and jewels. They were the most valuable and the easiest to fence.

One of them headed for the mezzanine, pulling a cut-down baseball bat and a sack out of his belt as he ran. The other one, the one with the gun, grabbed a rack of furs worth three-quarters of a million dollars and wheeled it down the aisle to the waiting van.

Then glass started breaking. The guy with the bat, up on the mezzanine, raced from jewelry case to jewelry case, smashing the glass and grabbing handfuls of jewels—diamonds, rubies, emeralds—to throw into his sack. The sound of smashing glass seemed to fill the room.

Karla was staring at her stopwatch. "One minute," she shouted over the din. The two looters seemed to pick up speed. Every few seconds a display case exploded, glass flying like spray from a wave. Two more racks of furs whizzed by her and out the back door to the waiting van.

As the seconds ticked away, Karla remained cool. "Thirty seconds!"

More jewels poured into the sack. Another rack of furs went out the back.

"Fifteen seconds!" Karla's voice had tightened a notch.

On the floor, Nancy was sure she was about to lose her mind. She was becoming unraveled—the smashing of the glass, the mystery woman's cold voice, it was all driving her mad. In spite of herself, she started to cry, the thick carpeting muffling her sobs. But Raul, next to her, heard them, and instinctively put out a hand to comfort her. Karla saw the gesture from the corner of her eye.

She cocked the gun. "One twitch," she hissed, "and you can kiss your head good-bye."

Raul decided Nancy didn't need comforting.

Everyone almost jumped out of their skin when Karla yelled: *"Time!"*

Everything stopped, except for Nancy's crying. The guy on the mezzanine grabbed his sack and headed down the stairs, taking them four at a time. In the alley there was the sound of the van starting up. Karla stepped away from Raul and Nancy and stood behind the guy with the gun. She nodded at him and his smile behind the mask was twisted and grotesque. This was the fun part, the part he had been waiting for. The stealing, that had been work. Now for some relaxation. He slid the gun out of the holster. It was a .44 auto mag. It could stop a truck.

Without a second's hesitation, he opened fire on the elegant shop. Chrome fixtures exploded off the walls. Expensive clothing in mahogany closets was ripped to shreds. Perfume cases blew out, filling the room with a dozen rare and exotic scents, mingling with the acidic smell of the burnt cordite. Cackling, he turned his cannon on the chandelier, and crystal chips, raining down like snow, flew off the giant light fixture. With each resounding boom of the big gun, the terrified people on the floor flinched and tried to burrow deeper into the carpet.

A couple of big slugs sliced into the mooring that held the chandelier to the ceiling. There were some sparks as the electric lines gave way and the entire tower of crystal crashed to the floor, shattering into millions of pieces.

Still he continued to blast away, as if not quite satisfied with the job he had done. Shell casings started piling up at his feet as he blasted the walls, the stairs, the displays, tearing Adriano's elegant interior to shreds. It was as if he were trying to pull the place down around them. Finally, Karla nudged him. That was enough. He was a perfectionist but reluctantly, he stopped. Suddenly the room was deathly still.

Karla stepped over a mound of broken glass and placed an envelope on the floor in front of Raul.

"When the cops get here," she said softly, "give them this." The envelope had a large block letter *A* on the front.

Then she was gone. They were all gone. But nobody moved. Nobody dared to. They heard the van drive away, but still they didn't move.

From the balcony a sliver of glass fell and bounced noiselessly on the carpet.

Later, they would all be surprised when they realized that the longest event of their lives had taken just six minutes. More astonishingly, no one had been hurt. Except for Francesco, of course.

Antoine felt shitty for weeks because he thought, really, that he should have done something heroic instead of just lying there sniveling like a jerk.

CHAPTER
THREE

Beverly Hills—the Beverly Hills Police Department included—had never heard of, never even conceived of, anything like the raid on Adriano's. Stores, even ones as exclusive as that chic boutique, had been robbed before. But to have a place hit, stripped bare, and trashed, in six minutes, in broad daylight in front of half a dozen witnesses—well, things like that just didn't happen in Beverly Hills. As far as Bogomil knew, they didn't happen anywhere.

And to crown it all, the raiders had left a calling card: that envelope with the big letter *A* on the front; it suggested that there would be a *B* raid and *C* raid and so on down the alphabet until they were stopped. The message contained in the envelope didn't give the B.H.P.D. much to go on.

Bogomil, as the man in charge of the investigation, stared at the message—if that was the right word for it. It was a cryptogram, a fourteen-digit sequence of numbers, a code of some kind, that either told them everything or nothing at all. The problem was cracking it.

Bogomil didn't know where to begin. But thin, nervous, always-ready-to-help Detective Billie Rosewood had had an idea, and already—as most of Rosewood's ideas turned out—it had landed them in hot water.

Billie peered around the door of Bogomil's cramped office. His partner, stocky and powerfully built, stood behind him.

"Uh, sir," said Rosewood tentatively.

Bogomil looked up sharply. "What is it, Rosewood?"

Billie was doing his best to be helpful. "Uh, the *L.A. Times* got a letter just like that about two hours ago." He pointed at the cryptogram that lay on Bogomil's desk.

His middle-aged, more experienced—but still cautious—partner Taggart rolled his eyes. "He knows that already, Billie."

Billie swallowed. "Oh."

Bogomil looked back at the letter. It read: 17-01-19-10-09-05-25-13-01-25-23-17-01-02. Now what the hell did that mean? He rubbed his eyes and pushed the letter away. He looked up at Billie. Rosewood shifted uneasily on his feet.

"Why did you get involved in this, Rosewood?" Bogomil was doing his best to control his anger.

Rosewood thrust his hands into his pockets, determined to stand his ground. Working with Axel Foley had changed Rosewood a little. He wasn't content to go by the book anymore. It didn't get you anywhere.

"Listen, Captain, I just thought I knew how to crack this code . . . I had this friend . . ." Rosewood's resolve dried up a little sooner than he had expected it to. It must have been the look on Bogomil's face that did it.

"This is not your case," said Bogomil forcefully.

"I had already assigned you and Taggart to the Peterson extortion case."

Rosewood opened his mouth to reply—he wasn't sure what he was going to say yet—but he never got a chance to say a word. Harold Lutz, the red-faced, irascible police chief—the brand-new chief of police of the city of Beverly Hills—came thundering into Bogomil's office like a small fat freight train.

Lutz was boiling mad and he wanted everyone to know it. "Bogomil," he barked, ignoring Rosewood and Taggart, "you and your men. In my office. Now!" Lutz stomped off down the hall.

Andrew Bogomil sighed, stood up, and put on his jacket. The old chief had been tough, but he had been fair. Lutz was nothing more than a little self-important tyrant. Where the old chief would not play favorites, Lutz did nothing but; where his predecessor would not tolerate ass-kissing, Lutz went out of his way to encourage it. He was going to make the B.H.P.D. over in his own image. And any cop on the force who didn't like it that way was free to go. A lot had already. A lot had been fired too.

"Come on, you two," said Bogomil to Taggart and Rosewood. "You heard the chief. In his office."

"Can't keep God waiting," mumbled Rosewood.

Bogomil turned on him, his eyes blazing with anger. "I don't want to hear that kind of talk, Rosewood."

Taggart knew he shouldn't open his mouth, but he did anyway. "Come on, Captain. He's fired or forced out every cop from the old days. The three of us are all that's left."

It was by-the-book Bogomil who spoke. "He's the

chief of this department," he said sternly, "and as long as he is, Sergeant, you keep your bellyaching to yourself."

Taggart nodded, stifling his own anger. "Yes, sir."

Bogomil walked briskly down the carpeted hallway, Taggart and Rosewood following. As they passed through the detectives' squad room, the men sitting there watched them pass, each of them thinking heaven that he was not in Bogomil, Rosewood, or Taggart's shoes.

"Very smart!" hissed Taggart at Rosewood. "*You* know how to crack this code! Are you crazy?"

Rosewood tried to make his partner understand just what he had tried to do. "Listen . . . unofficial friendships are very important to a street cop."

Taggart stopped dead in his tracks. He looked at his partner amazed. "Street cop? *Street cop?* Who the hell do you think you are? Axel? We weren't even *working* on this case."

Rosewood refused to be drawn. He tried to settle things down before they got to Lutz's office. He made a hash of it. "Come on, Taggart, I know you have troubles at home," he said soothingly. "But you must quiet down your busy mind. Mellow out a bit."

Taggart looked at his partner as if he were crazy.

Billie didn't notice. "These things work out. Trust me."

"Oh," said Taggart gruffly, "*now* I feel much better."

"Told you," said Billie, following Bogomil into Lutz's office. Taggart just shook his head and followed.

Lutz was behind his huge desk doing his best not to bite his unlit cigar in two. The only thing keeping him remotely in check was the fact that the mayor of Beverly Hills, Theodore Egan, was also in the room, talking on the phone. Walter Biddle, Lutz's chief brownnoser, sat on a couch, tingling with anticipation. He couldn't wait to hear Bogomil and his buddies bawled out.

He didn't have long to wait. Lutz tore into Rosewood first.

"You *moron*," Lutz barked. Everyone in the room winced. The mayor put his hand over the mouthpiece of the phone. Rosewood paled. "You called a *supervising agent* of the goddam FBI to help break these alphabet codes? This is a *local* crime and *my men* will solve it. Is that clear, Roseweed?"

"Actually, my name isn't Roseweed, sir. It's—"

"Shut up," snapped Lutz.

Lutz picked up a copy of the alphabet letter and tossed it at Bogomil.

"And *you!*" His voice was as loud as a pistol shot. Bogomil faced him, calm on the outside, but mad as a hornet inside. "Captain Bogomil, you were in charge of this investigation."

Biddle looked as happy as kid on the last day of school.

Lutz had lowered his voice to a lethal hiss. "Did you *order* Roseweed to—"

Rosewood decided that he would help out again. "Sir, Captain Bogomil didn't call the FBI. I did." It had not been a good idea. . . .

Lutz turned a deeper shade of red. He wanted to

hear Bogomil admit to the mistake. "Shut up," he shouted.

"Captain Bogomil didn't know anything about it," Rosewood persisted, shuffling his feet back and forth on the floor.

Lutz's eyes swiveled back to Rosewood like the guns on a battleship. "I said, *shut up*." Lutz quickly rethought his plan to get rid of Bogomil. If he hadn't gone to the FBI, then he would still have to take the heat for it. Those two buffoons, Rosewood and Taggart, could wait. It was Bogomil's skin he wanted. Lutz knew that Bogomil was twice the cop he would ever be. It was Bogomil who should be sitting behind the chief's desk. Lutz had to get rid of him quick. He was too much of a threat.

"So Roseweed called the FBI and you didn't know a damn thing about it." He pounded his fist on the desk. "Well, that cuts it." He shook his head, as if disgusted. "How can you consider yourself a commanding officer when you can't even maintain a supervisory relationship with your own men? You've been a negative element in this department ever since I took over, Andrew. Now you've superseded the chain of command." Lutz paused a moment before delivering his final blow. "As of this moment, you are suspended."

The mayor quietly hung up the phone. There was silence in the room. Rosewood felt his stomach turn over. This was his doing. Bogomil couldn't quite believe what he had heard. His jaw dropped. Lutz and Biddle beamed. Taggart wished he was someplace else.

Bogomil recovered first. "On what grounds?" he said evenly.

Lutz sounded as if he were quoting from a rule book. "Failure to have any knowledge or control over your personnel."

Bogomil's anger flared up hot. "Goddammit, Harold, I may have something—"

"Stop shouting," bellowed Lutz. "And you call me Chief Lutz, Captain." He glanced at the mayor. "This robbery could be a political disaster for the mayor and for me too. I won't have this investigation bungled by your incompetence."

Bogomil stared out the window, doing everything in his power to avoid adding "assaulting a police officer"—the chief at that—to the trouble he was already in.

"Policy requires us to allow you a board of review within two days," said Lutz in a calmer tone of voice. "I think that can be arranged." He turned to Taggart and Rosewood. They could use a little humiliation before he got rid of them too. "You two. Traffic duty. Let's see if you can handle double parking and leave the serious crimes to those more qualified."

Rosewood was about to say something, but Taggart jabbed him savagely in the ribs.

"Biddle!"

Biddle sat up straight. "Yessir!"

"You are in charge now."

Biddle smirked at Bogomil, Rosewood, and Taggart. "Yessir, thank you, sir," he said as if he were a marine in training camp.

"I want this crime solved fast," Lutz said. "The media is going to be screaming crime wave. And I won't have it." He pounded the desk again. "Get out and analyze the ink in that letter."

"Yessir, Chief Lutz."

Lutz scowled at the three other police officers in the room. "Bogomil, Roseweed, Taggart, get the hell out of here."

Bogomil walked away, leaving Taggart and Billie standing in the hall outside the chief's office. Taggart looked at Billie and shook his head. " 'These things work out,' huh, Billie?" he said sarcastically. "Trust me. They don't."

Andrew Bogomil had no place to go but home. He slid behind the wheel of his green Olds Cutlass and pulled out into traffic. He was already planning what he was going to say to the review board. He had twenty years in the Beverly Hills Police Department and never a blot on his record. He had a wall full of citations in his office and at home. He had dozens of major crimes solved under his belt. But Andrew Bogomil was no fool. He knew that Lutz had to get rid of him and he would use any means at his disposal to do it. The review board would vote exactly the way Lutz told it to.

As Bogomil swung his car onto El Camino, he shook his head dejectedly. In a couple of days he just might find himself out of a job. . . .

He was deep in thought, driving mechanically, hardly noticing the cars around him or even the neighborhood he was passing through. He was on automatic pilot, just following the usual route home, the one he had taken for years. He couldn't escape the strange feeling that his recent discoveries way up in the hills had something to do with the bizarre robbery at Adriano's. It was his old cop instinct flaring up again. But how did they fit together? He wrestled with the knot, completely oblivious to the black Mustang that cruised by him and to the brunette at the wheel looking over to make sure it was him.

She accelerated past him, and a mile or so farther on she pulled over to the curb. She threw open the hood and waved at the next car that passed— coincidentally, Andrew Bogomil in his green Oldsmobile. Bogomil was a gentleman of the old school. Here was the classic lady in distress. He decided to forget his own troubles for a moment and see if he couldn't help this lady out of hers. He slowed and pulled to the curb.

The brunette's looks took Bogomil's breath away. Her long dark hair and her perfect features worked their magic on him, much as they had on Raul just that morning. But Bogomil was a little cooler about it.

"Trouble?" he said as he got out of his car.

"It just stopped," she said. "I don't know a damn thing about cars."

Bogomil peered under the hood. He checked the points and made sure the carburetor wasn't blocked. He shrugged. "I don't see anything wrong, ma'am," he said, straightening up. But Karla wasn't paying any attention. She was making sure that the black Trans-Am was in position.

The big black car had pulled alongside them across the street and the window glided down.

Karla handed Bogomil an envelope. "What do you make of this, darling?"

Bogomil glanced at the envelope. Then he stared hard. There was a big *B* stamped on it. He looked up at the woman. She smiled back. He looked down at the envelope again. It was an alphabet letter, for Christ's sake. And the woman fit the description of the leader of the raid on Adriano's. But before he could react, the barrel of a .357 magnum poked out the window of the Trans-Am.

"Bye, Andrew," said Karla.

In the quiet residential neighborhood, the boom of the gun rattled windows for blocks. Andrew Bogomil felt the hot slap of a bullet burrowing into his shoulder. The force of the shot threw him back onto the hood of the Mustang. He slid to his knees, fighting against the pain in an effort to pull his gun from its holster.

Another shot rang out, blasting the window out of the Mustang and showering him with glass. He sprang for the woman, grabbing Karla by the hair. Her scalp pulled loose in his hand, making him stumble backward. He stared hard at his hand. He was clutching a fistful of wig. Amazed, he looked up at the woman. Her hair was long and blond. She had lost her dark glasses in the commotion—she had eyes as blue as the Caribbean. A third shot rang out and this one hit home. It slammed into Bogomil's chest, throwing him back to the curb. He didn't move.

Karla grabbed her wig and the dark glasses and

ran, cursing the whole way, behind the Mustang. *Nice shooting,* she thought. A Mustang with its window shot out wasn't going to look *too* suspicious. Not in Beverly Hills.

She slammed the car into gear, gave it all the gas it could take, and took off, fishtailing away from Bogomil's inert body in a cloud of burning rubber.

CHAPTER
FOUR

It was time, Axel Foley decided, to get out there and rid the Motor City of the criminal element. He had an appointment with the credit-card forgers at his "place of business," a warehouse on the other side of town that made the detectives' squad room look worse than it did already.

As Axel crossed the crowded room, he was pounced on by Jeffrey Friedman, another detective. Friedman had more trouble finding girls to date than he did running down crooks. Axel had made the mistake of introducing him to a friend of his, Beverly, and Jeffrey had immediately taken the poor girl on the worst date of her life. Axel was not glad to see Jeffrey bearing down on him.

"Jeffrey," Axel shouted, "I told you already. Beverly told me that you shouldn't call her, shouldn't try to see her, shouldn't even think about her. She never wants to see you again. Ever. Got it?"

"Never mind that, Axel," babbled Jeffrey, "Inspector Todd wants to see you immediately. I just wanted to warn you so he didn't catch you unaware" —Jeffrey didn't pause for breath—"what do you mean she doesn't want to talk to me?"

Axel stopped and looked pityingly at Jeffrey. "You know, Jeffrey, when I get really messed up, I try to imagine what it must be like to be trapped inside your head."

Jeffrey didn't appear to have heard. "Whenever Todd asks me about you, I always tell him that you are working twenty-four hours a day." Jeffrey changed gears abruptly. "Jeez, is that a Patek Philip watch? Listen, if there's ever any way I can help you with your undercover work—"

"Jeffrey," Axel ordered, "don't speak to me. Will you please stop speaking to me?"

That too made no impression on Jeffrey. He changed the subject again. "Look, if I can't call Beverly, then maybe you can give her my number in case she ever wants, you know, to go out with me again." His mouth ran on like a runaway train. "Is there anything I can do to get in on your under-cover thing? Is there anything I can do to help? Let me be in on it. Please, Axel, I could help you."

"No, Jeffrey."

"Listen, Axel, if there is something about me that Beverly didn't like, look, I thought her mother was kind of cute. Maybe . . ."

Axel fled toward the door, Jeffrey right behind him. "Look, Jeffrey, just tell Todd I'm on my way to make that fake credit-card bust. I'll talk to him later. Cover for me, will you?"

"I will," said Jeffrey, "if you promise to talk to Beverly."

Axel wheeled around. "Jeffrey," he said very calmly, "I have decided to shoot you in the leg. Are you ready?"

A brief spontaneous round of applause sprang up

45

in the squad room. "Good idea, Axel," shouted Orvis.

"Axel . . ." persisted a now-whining Jeffrey as Foley beat it out of there double quick.

The Ferrari carried him across town in fifteen fun-filled minutes. He pulled up in front of the Yum-Yum Puppy Chow Warehouse, the home of Axel's crime empire. He had a little office upstairs: a desk, a chair, a phone, and a TV set. Axel sat in the creaking chair, put his feet on the desk, and glanced at his beautiful watch. *Shit,* he thought. The meeting had been set up for four o'clock—and it was 4:30 already.

He leaned forward to turn on the TV set. "I hate crooks that are late," he said to the bare walls.

The black-and-white image of a newscaster came on the screen. Axel didn't pay too much attention to it until he heard a familiar name.

". . . Bogomil was gunned down in broad daylight." Axel sat bolt upright in his chair. How many Bogomils could there be in the world?

"The policeman, a captain with the Beverly Hills Police Department, was shot earlier this morning. Reports say he is alive but in critical condition. Captain Bogomil was in charge of the unit investigating the spectacular robbery of Adriano's, an exclusive Beverly Hills boutique, a crime that has already been dubbed the Alphabet Robbery, because of . . ."

But Axel wasn't listening anymore. He had lunged for the phone and dialed a number. It was answered on the first ring.

"Beverly Hills Police Department."

Axel kept his voice low. His forged credit-card contact could come through the door any minute and he didn't want to be caught talking to a police department even if it was half a continent away.

"Hi, Sheila," he said, "this is Axel Foley. You remember, from . . . Detroit, that's right. Look, I just heard about Andrew and I wonder if you could patch me through to his hospital room real quick? Thank you."

He waited a moment, glanced at his watch, looked out the window and down the hall. No sign of D'Allessio, the crook with the phony credit cards to sell.

Jan's tear-filled voice came on the line. "Axel?"

"Jan? What happened? How is he?"

"They're operating on him, Axel. . . ." There was a long silence and then a sob. "Look," she said, "I'm sorry, Axel, I can't talk anymore. . . ." He could tell that she was on the edge of breaking down. "Here's Billie, okay?"

Rosewood's voice filled Axel's ear. He sounded down, sad, sick at heart. "Axel?"

"Billie, what the hell happened?"

"This guy really nailed him. Set him up. Cold blood."

"Who?" Axel demanded. "Who? Who nailed him?"

"This Alphabet bandit."

"Billie? Are you on it?"

Rosewood's disgust came through loud and clear. "No. Neither is Taggart. It's not the same here, Axel. It's all politics."

Axel glanced up. Two thugs appeared in the

doorway. That was one more thug than Axel had expected. Next to D'Allessio stood a man who looked vaguely familiar. Axel looked at him closely. It was a guy Axel had tried to nail once with a truckload of stolen cigarettes. *Shit.*

D'Allessio smiled crookedly at Axel. "Jeez, I'm sorry I'm late. I ran into this broad . . ."

Axel's whole manner changed. He went from being a cop concerned about a fellow cop and a friend to being a street-wise criminal with heavy black accent to match. "I'll be with you in a minute," he shouted at D'Allessio. Then he turned back to the phone and spoke in his new accent to Rosewood. Billie thought he was talking to somebody else.

"It's an interesting proposition," said Axel, "but I think I better deal with it in person, know what I'm saying?"

"Axel? Is that you?" asked a very bewildered Rosewood.

"Take care of Jan," said Axel, hoping that would tell Rosewood that yes, it was still Axel Foley on the line, just that he was speaking in a different voice. Sometimes Rosewood was *so* dense. "I'll get over there right away."

"Get over where? Axel? Are you coming *here?*"

Rosewood got a click and a dial tone for an answer.

Mirsky, D'Allessio's pal, was looking at Axel closely. "I know this guy."

"Yeah?" said D'Allessio. "Where from?"

Mirsky was obviously taking a trip down memory lane. It would be hard to forget that wild ride in the cigarette truck. "This is the cigarette guy. Nearly got me fuckin' busted. You said you were from Buffalo."

"*I* got busted," said Axel, outraged. "*And* I lost my entire investment thanks to this man." He turned on D'Allessio. "What is going on here, man? I'm a businessman, you understand?"

"Yeah," said D'Allessio, "I understand that."

"I got a heavy schedule," Axel went on. Since speaking to Billie, a little credit-card bust was no longer that big a deal to him. He wanted to go find who had taken down his friend Andrew. Right now all he wanted was to get rid of these guys and head west. Fast.

"Yeah, I'm sorry. Like I said, I met this broad—"

"I'm late for my next meeting right now. I got business to do. I can't be hanging around waiting for you all day."

"Yeah, yeah . . ."

"And *then* you show up with the law," said Axel, jabbing a finger at D'Allessio. "I have no time for this bullshit."

D'Allessio looked as if he had just been tapped with a tire iron. He looked at Mirsky. "The law? What the hell is he talking about?"

"I'm talking about your pal, Dirty Harry here." He poked Mirsky in the chest.

Mirsky looked offended. "You calling me a cop?"

"You got it," said Axel bluntly.

"You're nuts, man," bellowed D'Allessio. "This is my fuckin' nephew."

Axel didn't crack a smile. "Hey, man, you can choose your friends but you can't choose your family."

"Don't give me that, man," said D'Alessio. "My nephew ain't no cop. He's stand-up, trust me."

Axel patted Mirsky on the back. "Maybe he's not a cop. Maybe he's just bad luck."

Mirsky looked pissed. "Carlotta's doing one-to-five in the prison body shop fixing all the cars he wrecked, and he calls me . . ."

Axel had gone from patting Mirsky on the back to patting him down, as if looking for a weapon. The hood slapped Axel's hands away. "What the hell you doing, man?" he demanded angrily.

"Okay, he's not wearing a wire. That's something, I guess."

"A wire!" yelled Mirsky.

"Okay," said D'Alessio, "let's cut the shit. I got two thousand blank American Express cards. Gold cards. You got the money?"

The way Axel had planned it, it was at this point that he would have zoomed D'Alessio, closed down the phony credit-card operation and his undercover career. But the shooting of Andrew Bogomil had changed all that. If he took D'Alessio and—what the hell—Mirsky too, he would spend the next ten days cleaning up the case, huddling with prosecutors from the DA's office, and generally wasting time in courtrooms and before grand juries. All this while whoever shot his friend was getting away with it. No, the credit cards would have to wait. He whipped back into his act at full speed.

"I do no business in front of this man. He may be your nephew but—" Axel sniffed the air around Mirsky. "Pork! I definitely smell pork. Pig meat. I used to be a Muslim, man, so I know pork when I smell it." He pointed an accusing finger at Mirsky. "This man is the law." He turned to the astonished D'Allessio. "You want to do business with me, you come back by yourself. You know where to find me."

Axel got out of there quick because there was no mistaking the need to kill in Mirsky's eyes. D'Allessio, who was about two hundred pounds heavier than his nephew, held him back. As Axel retreated down the cavernous hallway of the dog-food warehouse, Axel could hear D'Allessio's voice: "Tell me for real, Paulie, you ain't no cop, are you?"

Axel beat it back to the squad room, his mind in overdrive. He had a little vacation time coming to him this year, but Todd wasn't going to let him take it now, not in the middle of a case. He had to figure out a plan to disappear for the few days he needed to get out to the coast—but at the same time he had to make it look like he was still in Detroit.

That part was easy. The most distinctive thing about Axel these days, the thing that people noticed most, was the Ferrari. If he kept that on the streets, people would think he was still here. *Now,* he thought, *who would be dumb enough . . .*

It was as if Jeffrey had not moved since Axel had left a hour before. He was waiting by the door and immediately got his mouth working when Axel walked in.

"Jesus, Axel, where you been? Todd's been going nuts trying to find you. Did you make the bust? Did you?"

Jeffrey, thought Axel, grinning to himself, Jeffrey would be dumb enough to take the Ferrari off his hands for a few days. He sat Jeffrey down at a desk.

"Axel, I said did you make the bust? You didn't make the bust, did you? Todd is going to go bullshit. That is one hell of a tie."

"Never mind that now," said Axel gravely, "I need you, I need to know if I can count on you."

Axel's sudden seriousness allowed Jeffrey to show off one of his rare moments of silence.

He paused and then spoke slowly. "Sure . . . To do what?"

Axel gripped Jeffrey by the shoulders. "I want you to take care of the Ferrari for a few days. I'm going to be out of town. I want you to drive it around."

"Drive the Ferrari?" said Jeffrey dubiously.

"But that's not important, Jeffrey." Axel was revving up his line of bullshit. "It's not important that in that car you can get any girl you want— maybe even Beverly. That's not important."

"It isn't?"

"No. What's important here is the bond that exists between cops. The trust between friends."

"Of course we have that," said Jeffrey. His mind was already full of dreams of that car: him, the car, Beverly. Or maybe the hell with Beverly, with a car like that . . . But there had to be a catch. Axel was up to something.

Jeffrey's eyes narrowed. *"Just* drive the Ferrari?" he asked suspiciously. "That's all?"

"Take care of it, and drive it around every day with the windows rolled up."

"With the windows rolled up? How come?"

"Because no one must know that it's you driving the Ferrari. Not even Todd."

Jeffrey swallowed hard. "What about Beverly?"

"Beverly will be in the car with you," Axel explained patiently. "I'm talking about people outside the car. You can talk to no one outside the car while you're driving it. Do you understand?"

Jeffrey told the truth: "No."

Axel told the truth: "That's good. You'll understand when you need to understand. This is an important job, Jeffrey. Can you handle it?"

Axel could see Jeffrey's mind working. *Drive the Ferrari with the windows rolled up and don't talk to anyone on the street while I'm driving.* How could he screw that up? "You can count on me, Axel."

"If this operation goes down right, I'll be going straight to the top, and I'm taking you with me. How's that?"

Right at that moment, Jeffrey didn't give a damn about advancing his career in the Detroit P.D. *"Just drive the Ferrari?"*

"And don't tell anybody, not even Todd. And don't let anything happen to that car."

Jeffrey put his hand on his heart. "I'll guard it with my life."

"Your life wouldn't cover the cost of a dent in the fender." Axel dangled the keys tantalizingly above Jeffrey's head. "I can trust you, right?"

"Absolutely," said Jeffrey firmly.

Axel tossed the keys down on the desk. "It's parked downstairs."

Jeffrey picked up the keys and looked at them as if they could unlock the gates of heaven.

Captain Todd's office was the size of two phone booths and it was jammed with a couple of filing cabinets and a desk that was so battered it looked like it had been dropped several stories before finding a home with Todd.

Todd was not pleased to see Axel standing in the doorway of his office, all dressed up in his department-bought clothes. Todd had been looking for Axel for hours, and now that he was here, he wasn't glad to see him at all. The part he particularly didn't care for was the little blue slip of paper that Foley held in his hand.

"Where the goddamn hell you been, Foley? And what the hell is that blue slip for?" He whipped the requisition form out of Axel's hand. He stared at it so hard it looked as if he was trying to kill it with his eyes. "What do you need a thousand dollars for!"

"Flash money," Axel said calmly. "It says so right there on the slip."

Growling, Todd yanked open the top drawer of one of his filing cabinets. The action almost toppled over the picture of his wife and kids that sat there. He pulled out a fistful of blue requisition slips.

He read them off, tossing them one by one on his desk in front of Axel. "Two thousand for a suit. Three hundred dollars for a fucking tie. A requisition order for a Ferrari. I don't want any more of these blue slips. I'm up to my ass in blue slips. When the hell am I gonna see some *booking* slips?"

"Inspector," said Axel earnestly, "I am so close to a major bust I can smell it."

"I don't give a shit what you smell, Foley," said Todd in a voice about as inviting as a band-saw. "For six months I've been pouring money down a bottomless rat hole. Where's the bad guys at the end of the rainbow?"

"Inspector," said Axel seriously, "if you don't feel I'm doing my job adequately, I'll go back to Robbery-Homicide."

Todd's eyes blazed. How much shit was he going to take from this man? But Todd was as deep in the operation as Foley was. Foley knew it too.

"*I* tell *you* where to go, Foley. *You* don't tell *me*!"

Axel knew he had him. "I just thought—"

"Don't think, Foley," Todd commanded. "It makes my pecker twitch." He looked down at the sheaf of blue slips on his desk. "The department's fronted you a goddamn fortune. My ass is on the line. I okay'd all this shit." He tossed a handful of blue slips in the air like confetti. "I can't pull out of this till I get some kind of bust or my fucking career is finished." He looked hard and mean at Axel. "But I promise you, I won't go down alone. I'm giving you three days. If I don't see results by then, I'm going to cover my own ass. I'm going to pull the pin and let you take the heat. You got any problems with that arrangement?"

It suited Axel perfectly, but not quite in the way the inspector had in mind. "Fair enough, Inspector. But since you've only given me three days, I'll have to go deep, deep, deep undercover. You won't be able to reach me or page me or anything. And I probably won't be able to call in."

"I am tired of your bullshit, Foley. I don't care if I never hear from you again. You got three days to come up with the bodies. You don't have a bust by then, I'll grind your ass to dog meat. You got that?"

"I believe that's clear. Now if you'll just sign that slip for the flash money . . ."

Muttering, Todd scribbed his signature on the slip. "Flash money . . . and God help you if anything happens to that Ferrari. That's a fifty-thousand-dollar automobile."

"Sixty-seven thousand five hundred, actually, sir."

"You just better make sure that nothing happens to it."

"I'll never let it out of my sight. I'll keep it under my pillow at night. No, better, I'll sleep *in* it. Have meals sent in. Get a bedpan . . . Nobody will drive it but me."

"That's what I'm afraid of." Todd tossed the blue slip at Axel. "You spend a cent of that money and you make up the difference out of your own pocket. Now get the hell out of here."

Axel got the hell out, wondering how much of the flash money he'd need for a cheap flight to California.

CHAPTER
FIVE

Axel caught a flight out of Detroit at six and, what with the time difference and everything, arrived in Los Angeles at about the same time he left. That struck him as weird.

The first thing he needed was a car. Without a car in Los Angeles, you were nothing. Briefly, he regretted not having brought the Ferrari—it probably would have been faster than flying—but it was too late for that now.

Axel got a good deal on a rental car at Rent-A-Wreck—a long, sleek, Caddy Eldorado that didn't have too many dings in it. The black smoke that poured out of the tailpipe didn't even last once you got over thirty miles an hour.

He swung the mammoth machine through the wide, clean streets of Beverly Hills, reacquainting himself with the city. He passed the Beverly Palm Hotel where he had stayed the last time he was here. He wasn't altogether sure that the B.H.P.D. would pay the bill again, so he passed the luxurious hotel by. Besides, he already had three of their bathrobes.

He paused at a light on Wilshire and a Red Ferrari Testa Rossa glided up next to him. Axel rolled down his window and looked over at the middle-aged man behind the wheel. "Hey, yo, mister," Axel called out, pleasure in his voice, "I got one just like that back home in Detroit."

The man ran his eyes disdainfully over the dented Eldorado. And gave Axel a look that said: "*Sure* you do, buddy."

Just then the light changed and Axel zoomed forward, burying the Ferrari in a cloud of dirty, oily smoke. Axel shook his head. If you don't know how to drive a Ferrari, then why buy a Ferrari?

Axel swung left, then right, looking at the palm trees, the suntanned rich people and their amazing automobiles. This was some kind of town. . . .

"Maybe I'll retire here," he said aloud.

The hospital wasn't far from the headquarters of the Beverly Hills Police. Axel pulled the Eldorado into the parking lot and jumped out. A few minutes later, the elevator doors slid open and Axel was on the intensive-care-unit floor. The first person he saw was Rosewood.

"Billie!"

When Axel had said on the phone that he would be right over, Rosewood couldn't bring himself to believe it. But here he was.

"Axel! What the heck are you doing here?" Rosewood's face was one goofy, goodhearted grin.

The two uniformed policemen who were guarding the door of Bogomil's room looked up from their magazines. Rosewood glanced at them nervously, the smile wiped off his face, and backed Axel a little way down the hall.

"What am I doing here? You guys got a problem. I'm here. Now tell me how he's doing."

Rosewood shook his head. "He's right on the

edge. They repaired the artery in his shoulder. He's got a chance. He's strong as a bull."

Axel nodded. The lightheartedness was gone. In the next room a friend of his was dying and he was going to do something about it.

Taggart came down the hall and shook Axel's hands. The two men smiled at one another.

"Can he talk?" Axel asked in a low voice.

Taggart shook his head. "No. They say he's out for a week at least."

"I want to see him. Get me in there."

Taggart and Rosewood hesitated, but Axel didn't. He walked down the hall toward the guards, ready to talk, or beat, his way in. Rosewood caught up with him just in time. He jerked a thumb at Axel.

"He's a relative, guys."

The guards looked at Axel. "But Rosewood, he's black."

"Believe me," said Rosewood sincerely.

"It's the truth," said Axel.

"And the captain is white," said the other guard. "So how can he be a relative?"

"I'm a distant, very distant relative. On his step-father's side."

"Oh," said the policeman. The two of them exchanged glances and shrugged. Reluctantly, they let him in. Axel turned in the doorway. "Can I look at the letters the guy left?"

Rosewood and Taggart came up close and spoke in whispers.

"They're at the station," said Billie.

"We can't take you there. We're not even sup-posed to be working on the Alphabet case." Taggart

BEVERLY HILLS COP II

paused and wiped his brow. "It's a new ballgame out here. We weren't invited."

"Me neither," said Axel, "but I'm playin' anyway."

"Look," whispered Rosewood, "it wouldn't hurt just to let him *see* the letters."

Taggart sighed heavily. "Okay," he said reluctantly. He knew it was the wrong thing to do. He also knew that Axel would find a way to see the evidence without them. Taggart figured it was safer being with Axel than having him operate on his own. "But listen, Axel, you don't have jurisdiction here. Lutz would love a chance to bust our asses."

"Lutz?" asked Axel. "What's a Lutz?"

"Lutz is a who," whispered Rosewood. "He's the new chief."

"I can't wait to meet him."

"If I were you, I could wait a long time," growled Taggart.

Axel nodded. "Meet me at the station in an hour."

He stepped into the ICU. The lights were dim and the only sound was the rhythmic pumping of the respirator and the beeping of the EKG. Andrew Bogomil could be seen through a glass partition lying on a bed. His skin was deathly white, as if all the blood had been drained from him. One arm was wrapped in a cuff and a tube protruded from it. Another tube was attached to his nose. Tubing seemed to snake all over the room, leading from various machines into Bogomil's body. That was all that was keeping him alive.

Jan was staring through the glass, her pretty face

drawn and tearstained. Axel touched her lightly on the shoulder. "Hi, kid," he said softly.

She looked up. "Hi, Axel," she whispered, as if she might awaken her father.

Axel looked at Andrew and felt his heart sink. Bogomil was hurt bad. He would have to be every bit as strong as Rosewood said he was to pull through this. But Axel hid his concern.

"I get shot like this all the time in Detroit, Jan. He'll be fine."

Jan managed a ghost of a smile. Then she turned back to her father as if her vigilance was helping to keep him alive.

But Axel knew that Bogomil's life was in the hands of his doctors and Andrew's own will to live. He, on the other hand, couldn't do anything about saving Andrew's life. What he could do was make life as unpleasant as possible for the people who had put his friend here.

"What was he working on, Jan? Any ideas?"

She shook her head. "He was talking about going fishing until yesterday. Then . . ."

"Then what?"

Jan shrugged. "I don't know, it's hard to explain. All of a sudden he was so . . . so preoccupied. You know him, when he gets hold of an idea . . ."

Axel wet his lips. "Yeah, but *what* idea?"

Again Jan shook her head. "I don't know. I'm sorry, Axel. I just don't know. . . ." She looked back at her father, her voice filled with tears and anguish. "I feel so helpless."

He put his arm around her to comfort her. "Lis-

ten, Jan," he whispered, "he's going to be okay.
That's a promise."

She nodded, but without much conviction. "I
know."

"Good. Look, I want to come by the house after I
get settled. I want to take a look at his office. Will
you be there?"

Jan nodded. "Yeah, I'll be heading home soon."

"See you later, then." He started for the door.
She caught him lightly by the wrist. "Axel," she said
tenderly, "thanks."

Axel nodded and shrugged. "What are friends
for?"

"It would mean a lot to him," she said, "if he
knew you were here."

Axel grinned. "Don't be so sure he doesn't know
—but if he doesn't, he's gonna find out the minute
he wakes up." Because, Axel swore to himself, he
was going to tear this town apart, if he had to. . . .

Axel drove the Cadillac down one of Beverly
Hills' wide, quiet streets, glancing from right to left
at the mansions that lined the road. There were so
many rooms in each of them he figured he could
probably live in one for a week before anyone
noticed him.

He drove past a mansion that had work crews
swarming all over it. Some of the windows were
boarded up and others had carpenters hanging half
out of them as they installed new frames. The place
was giant, all white, and as soon as the heavy
construction was finished, it was going to be an

impressive house, even for Beverly Hills. As he glided by, he saw the end of a sofa—still wrapped in heavy plastic—being carried through the wide double doors of the palatial house. If they were putting furniture in the place already, he reasoned, they must be close to finishing.

Abruptly he did a U-turn, swung around, and pulled into the driveway. The two furniture deliverers were coming down the steps, having dumped the couch in a big room they took to be the living room. Let the decorator figure out where it really should be.

Axel approached one of them. "Excuse me, I'm looking for the owners of this place."

"They're not here. They're in Hawaii for a week or so while the remodeling is going on."

"Lucky thing. Where's the foreman?"

"Hey, how the fuck should I know? I deliver furniture."

"Sorry man," said Axel, "sorry."

He walked up the steps to where a group of men were working. He folded his arms across his chest and surveyed the scene, as if he were a general watching troop maneuvers. He looked all around, getting down on one knee as he watched some of the workmen running out a line to guide the laying of a walkway around the side of the house.

Axel stood up. *"What* are you doing?" he yelled.

Workmen all over the site looked up, saw Axel, and looked at each other. "Who the hell is that guy?" one of them asked no one in particular.

"Stop! *Stop!*" Axel bellowed. "Everybody shut the fuck down."

Everyone stopped, a few of them dropping their tools as if Axel had a gun on them. The foreman came running.

"Who . . . ?" was all he had the chance to say.

"I'm Axel Foley, city of Beverly Hills, building inspection. You look like the foreman. I bet you can read."

"For years now."

"Good," ordered Axel. "Let's see the plans. Let's just see how you read plans."

"Larry, go get the plans," the foreman said to one of the workmen. "They're in the trailer in the back."

Axel looked around furiously, as if he couldn't believe his eyes. "Just my luck, I come by here for a routine inspection and what do I find?" He turned to the foreman. "My people were clear with your people . . . I was in the meeting. Were you in the meeting? Yeah, you were in the meeting—I remember your face."

The foreman felt a little sick. There *had* been a meeting. He hadn't gone to it—and now he had a building inspector climbing up his ass. "Meeting?"

"The second meeting," said Axel hotly. "Were you there?"

The foreman paled. A *second* meeting. There had been two meetings and he hadn't gone to that one either. Shit. "No . . . I mean, I don't remember."

"My boss heard it, the planning commissioner heard it, I heard it . . ."

"What? What did you hear?"

"No *right angles!*" Axel marched to a corner of the house and pointed accusingly at it. "What's this?"

The foreman chewed his lip. It was a corner, a fucking right angle. So what? You can't build a house without them. At least he didn't think so . . .

Axel answered the question for him. "It's a right angle. Isn't it?"

"Look . . . we weren't told—"

Axel interrupted, furious. "Answer the question."

The hapless foreman rubbed one foot against the other, like a sixth-grader called out in front of the entire class.

"Yes," he said finally.

"Yes what?" Axel raged at him. "Say the word, I want to hear you say the word."

"It's a right angle," he said quietly.

"*Exactly.*" Axel crossed his arms across his chest again and shook his head. "This is a major fuck-up, boys. I mean bad. Very bad . . ." The workmen looked nervously at Axel and then over at their foreman. "I could get fired . . . and you could get fired."

Something about all this struck the foreman as strange. "Wait a minute," he said, "this place will be round as a fucking donut if there are no right angles."

Axel fixed a withering gaze on him. "What are you? An art critic? Are you?"

"No, it's just that—"

Axel addressed all the workmen now. "Obviously you'll get your paycheck at the end of the week. Beyond that I can't make any promises. There may be something I can do. *Maybe.*"

"Wait a minute," began the foreman.

"Shut up. I'll have to talk to my people, they have to talk to their people, and *then* they'll talk to your people."

"But," said the foreman.

"Shut up. So for now . . . go home . . . pack your equipment, take off the rest of the week, drink beer, pork the old lady . . . whatever you do . . . and I'll *try* to straighten this out."

The workmen looked at Axel and at the foreman. Slowly they began packing up their tools, looking a little bewildered as they did so.

The foreman thrust the plans under Axel's nose. Axel glanced at them, reading the name of the owners of the house prominently displayed across the top of the blueprint.

"Look," said the foreman, pointing at the plans. "Right angles, all over the place. This house is lousy with them."

Axel pulled the plans out of the man's hand. "Old plans, old plans," he yelled. "You shouldn't have these. They need to be refiled. The Rosenbergs will shit. Who gave you these?"

Axel tore the plans into a dozen pieces and handed them back to the foreman. "I said, who gave you these?"

"I . . . don't remember."

But Axel was ignoring him now. He smiled broadly and waved at the departing workmen. They were straggling down the road like convicts who have been told by the warden that they didn't have to hang around the prison anymore.

"Except for these right angles," he shouted at them, "you've all done some beautiful work here. I

mean that. Give yourself a big hand. Seriously."
Axel began clapping. The workmen, looking back in
amazement, clapped raggedly.

"Don't feel bad," Axel said. "Think of this as a
vacation with pay. And you deserve it."

He turned back to the foreman. "You too. You're
a nice man and I like you. Anything else I should
know?"

"No . . . well, the decorator will be here later."

"I'll handle him for you."

"Yeah, well, okay. Good." The foreman looked at
his crew straggling away. "I guess there's no reason
for me to . . ."

"Take off," said Axel. "I'll handle everything."

Axel stood on the lawn and waited until the
foreman was out of sight. Then he got his suitcase
from the car and walked up the steps. He pushed the
door of the house open. Before him was a tiled
entrance hall that was the size of his whole apartment back in Detroit. He tiptoed into the giant living
room and looked through the floor-to-ceiling french
doors at the giant swimming pool in the large garden
beyond. The blue water twinkled in the bright
California sun.

Axel dropped his bag. "Home at last," he said.

CHAPTER
SIX

There were very few people in the plush squad room of the Beverly Hills Police headquarters when Axel showed up. Lutz had sent half the men under his command tearing all over greater Los Angeles trying to track down the origin of the paper and ink used in the messages left by the Alphabet bandit. He also had a squad of computer experts working at trying to break the codes. They were having no more luck than Axel, who was sitting at Taggart's desk writing the code out, fiddling with it, reversing the order of the numbers, not really expecting to get anything, but giving it a shot nonetheless.

"Lutz says he's a serial robber. Like a serial killer," said Taggart, "just robbing for the hell of it. A nut."

Rosewood snorted in derision. "Well, it's kind of obvious he's a nut, isn't it?"

"I don't think so," said Axel. He put his feet up on the desk. He was wearing his old uniform—blue jeans, sweatshirt, running shoes. Taggart looked down at Axel's feet.

"Axel, you want to get your feet off the desk?" he said nervously. "If Lutz . . ."

Axel swung his feet off the desk. "Man, I can't wait to meet this guy Lutz, he's got you all scared shitless."

70

"Right," said Taggart, "he has."

"Take a look at these, Axel," said Rosewood, handing him an evidence bag. "These are the shell casings left over from the robbery at Adriano's."

These made Axel sit up and take notice. *"Jesus.* Forty-four auto mag? They don't even make .44 auto mags anymore. Too expensive."

He slipped one of the slugs out of the plastic bag and studied it closely. "See, this is a .308 rifle-shell casing that's been cut to fit the .44." He whistled low. "Whoever put this gun together knew what he was doing. This is very nice work. *Very* nice." He glanced up at Taggart and saw two men coming down the hall toward them. "And who might this be?"

Rosewood and Taggart looked around. Neither of them noticed Axel slipping the spent shell into his jeans pocket.

"Oh shit," breathed Rosewood, "Lutz."

Lutz stopped and looked angrily in their direction. "What the hell are you doing?" he yelled.

"Chief," said Billie, "this is—"

"Shut up, Roseweed."

"Rosewood, Chie—"

But Axel cut him off, jumped to his feet, and extended a hand. "You must be Chief Lutz." Lutz didn't shake. "Quite an operation you got here," said Axel without pausing. "All the latest equipment. Very impressive." He looked at Biddle as if he were a trespasser. "And you are?"

"Captain Biddle," said Biddle.

"And who the hell are you?" demanded Lutz.

"Richard James with the U.S. marshal's office," Axel lied smoothly. Taggart and Rosewood looked out the windows.

"And what are you doing in my squad room?" bellowed Lutz. He rarely spoke in a tone of voice softer than a low roar. He thought it conferred authority on him.

"I came over to pick up a prisoner at the county jail and take him over to Terminal Island." Axel shook his head. "I always wanted to be a real cop, like these two. But I wound up moving bodies. I just stopped by to say hello."

"Have you said hello?" asked Biddle sarcastically.

"Yup. Nice meeting you guys." He looked around the room, taking in the sophisticated communications equipment and the nice potted plants that were placed here and there around the squad room. If they were in the Detroit P.D. detectives' squad room, they would have died of acid rain by now. "Very classy setup, Chief Lutz." He glanced at his watch. "Gotta go. Gotta move the meat. Prisoner's ready for transport. See you."

Axel strode out of the room as if he owned the joint.

Lutz watched him go, his distaste for the "marshal" showing plainly.

"Federal marshal's office needs a goddamn dress code." Then he turned on Rosewood and Taggart. "What the hell are you still doing here?"

Taggart grabbed for a lie and came up with one. "Uh . . . We're just finishing up our paperwork on the Peterson extortion case."

Something told Lutz not to believe this. "Listen,

Sergeant Taggart, you two are living on borrowed time. You are going to follow my goddamn orders and get out there on traffic or turn in your badges."

"The choice is yours," said Biddle, always the perfect toady.

"Get out of here," said Lutz.

They went. They left the building and headed toward their car. Both looked like down, almost broken men. Lutz was bad enough, but to have Bogomil fighting for his life in the ICU of a hospital —it was too much.

Taggart was rubbing his left arm, as if trying to soothe away a nagging pain. "I got angina the minute I saw Foley . . . Axel's got nine lives. I don't."

They turned a corner and there was Axel sitting on top of their cruiser. He grinned broadly and clapped his hands like a coach trying to rally his team. "Are you ready?"

Taggart and Rosewood just stared.

"No, see," said Axel, explaining patiently, "you are supposed to say, 'Yeah, c'mon, let's go get the Alphabet bandit.'"

"We are?" said Rosewood.

Axel looked disgusted with them both. "Come on, guys. That Lutz is a tinhorn shit-for-brains politician." Axel hopped off the car. "And *Biddle?* He couldn't stop the Alphabet bandit with nuclear weapons. We gotta run this thing into the ground here. The three of us . . . One for all? All for one?"

Taggart and Rosewood just stared, arms limp at their sides.

"Right. Look, I have only two days before I have

73

to be back in Detroit. I can't do it alone. We're gonna have to work fast before Lutz and Biddle piss all over the trail."

Taggart shook his head. "Axel, he'll fire our asses. I'll lose my pension. My medical . . . I got a wife and two kids to feed."

Rosewood rolled his eyes. "Now, come on, Sarge. You got two kids. Not a *wife* and two kids. You see, Axel, Maureen's divorcing him again. She's moved in with her mother."

Taggart didn't like to hear his personal life divulged, even to Axel. "Shut up, Billie. She might come back anytime."

Axel waved away all this talk. "Let's discuss what we owe Bogomil. Two years ago he broke all kinds of rules . . . and he saved my job. Now he's in the hospital unconscious. There's no way I'm going back to Detroit without trying to help him." He looked pleadingly, serious now, at Taggart. "Come on, man. Don't you think you owe Bogomil anything?"

Taggart and Axel locked eyes. Taggart looked away. This was more trouble than he had bargained on, but, yeah, he did owe Bogomil something—in fact, he owed him a lot.

"Okay," he said finally. "But I want to keep a low profile, dammit. It's gotta be covert. We're supposed to report to traffic."

Axel dug the .44 slug out of his pocket. Already Taggart knew he had made a mistake. "That's evidence, Axel. For God's sake, that stuff is cataloged and—"

"They had several. I only took one."

"What for?" asked Rosewood, mystified.

"In police work, Rosewood," said Axel, holding the casing up as if it were a jewel, "we call this a clue. Maybe you're familiar with the term. Now there can't be more than four or five guys in this city who can do this kind of quality work. I want to show this around and see who recognizes it."

Rosewood looked genuinely excited by Axel's deduction. "Good idea, Axel. Who are the three or four guys?"

Axel's shoulders slumped and he laughed a little. "Well, if this was Detroit, I could tell you. But I was kind of hoping you would know, this being your town."

"Oh," said Rosewood.

Taggart scratched his chin. "There's a guy at the Beverly Hills Shooting Club—Russ Fielding his name is—he's supposed to be the best."

"Good enough for starters. Let's go." Axel opened the door of their car.

"Well, you have to be a member to get in," Taggart said sheepishly.

Axel shook his head vehemently. "I'm sorry. I will *not* join that club. I don't mind going there, asking a few embarrassing questions—maybe have a little lunch. But I will not join."

"I don't think you're gonna have that problem," said Taggart. "Get in the car."

The Beverly Hills Shooting Club was a graceful mansion sitting in the middle of thirty acres of perfectly kept lawns and gardens. The firing ranges were all within the clubhouse building itself—it kept the noise down. The rest of the estate was given over to tennis courts and a small nine-hole golf course in case the select clientele wanted a little exercise after exercising their constitutional right to bear arms. As Axel peered through the gates, he got a good idea of what the place was like: rich gun nuts came here to shoot, play, and dine among their "own kind."

The whole place looked like money. Axel counted seven Bentleys and twelve Rolls Corniches in the parking lot. He had a feeling he would not be mistaken for a member if he just ambled in.

Taggart looked at the place with unconcealed awe. "God," he said, "that is one high-dollar place. Even for this town."

"Lutz and Mayor Egan are both members," piped up Rosewood.

Axel opened the back door of the car and got out. "That's okay," he said with a smile, "I don't mind slumming. You meet me at my house in an hour: 1603 Hillcrest. Big white house. You can't miss it."

Taggart pulled the car away from the curb but watched as Axel walked nonchalantly up the long driveway toward the club. "He's going in there," he said in amazement. He gave the car a little more gas. "Well, it's his ass, not ours."

Rosewood shook his head. "I don't think that's a very positive attitude, Sarge."

There was no denying that the receptionist in the plush lobby of the Beverly Hills Shooting Club was surprised when she looked up to see a poorly dressed young black man standing at her desk.

"May I help you?"

"I'm from the Metalux Explosive Research Company," said Axel. "Do you have a Mr. Russell Fielding working here?"

"Yes we do."

"Good. I have a delivery of plutonium nitrate multi-explosive sound-seeking projectiles that I'm supposed to drop off to Mr. Fielding."

The receptionist frowned down at her agenda. "I have no record of a delivery of that type."

Axel had taken the rounds out of his own Browning and he placed the nine mean-looking bullets one by one on the top of the secretary's desk, as if he were setting up a chessboard.

The secretary looked at them unhappily—she might work in a gun club but all bullets looked the same to her.

"Well," Axel said resignedly, "as usual, there's been a mix-up. You can call Metalux Research and clear it up. Me, I'm getting the hell out of here. I'm only paid to take them from A to B. This here club is B." He looked around the plush interior of the club. "Yeah, this is B, all right. I'll be damned if I'm going to get exploded 'cause some secretary fucked up." He looked down at the receptionist. "Let me give you a word of advice: when you take these things to the man . . ."

"Yes?"

"Don't sneeze, don't use the phone, and if you have gas, make sure it's a quiet one."

Axel turned on his heel and started for the door at a brisk pace, as if he wanted to get out of there fast. The receptionist stood up and called after him.

"Sir—"

Axel kept walking.

"Excuse me, sir. Excuse me—"

Axel stopped, turned around, and pointed at himself. "Me?" he asked, raising his eyebrows.

"Yes, sir, I was wondering if you could take them to Mr. Fielding for me."

Axel frowned. "Hey! I'm a delivery man. I get three-sixty-five to go from A to B. Not from B to C. I got a wife and three kids, lady. And I *had* this friend, Bootsie, that got exploded for some shit just like that. Maybe you read about it in the newspapers. It was bloody, pieces of Bootsie all over the place."

"Please," pleaded the receptionist, glancing at the bullets, "please take these bullets off my desk and give them to Mr. Fielding. He'll know what to do with them."

Axel crossed his arms and looked critically at the receptionist. "What's in it for me?"

"Oh," she said, burrowing in her purse, "of course . . ." She came up with ten dollars.

Axel turned his nose up. "Ten bucks! I got a wife and three girls, lady."

The receptionist dragged another ten out of her handbag.

He took the money out of her hand and swept the bullets up as if he were clearing crumbs off a tablecloth. The secretary winced.

"Twenty bucks, shit," he mumbled. "Risking my life for twenty bucks. That was all that was left of Bootsie. Twenty bucks and a pair of sneakers."

"I'm sorry about your friend."

"Yeah, me too, lady. Which way?"

She pointed across the lobby and watched him go with obvious relief.

Russ Fielding sat in the gun shop of the Beverly Hills Shooting Club, surrounded by the tools of his trade and by guns and ammo. Coincidentally, he was reading a magazine called *Guns and Ammo*. Axel looked at the sleek display cases admiringly. There were finely crafted Anschutz target rifles, good enough for world-class target events, hand-rubbed black walnut Winslows, deadly-looking Iver and Johnson carbines, a rack of lethal Heckler and Koch semi-automatics—just the kind of thing to have around the house if you were expecting the 101st Airborne. There was even a complete Uzi display: gun, stock, three clips. And it all fit in a nice little carrying case that said "Uzi" on the outside—perfect for fooling the customs man.

The only poorly designed item in the room was Russ Fielding himself. He was sitting behind the counter, a paunchy, unshaven, rather nearsighted man. His fat fingers didn't look capable of making the tiny, delicate maneuvers needed to build a bullet or calibrate a sight.

"You Russ Fielding? The gunsmith?"

Fielding looked up. "Yeah."

Axel put the .44-auto-mag casing on the counter in front of Fielding. "You ever see one of these, Russ?"

He scarcely glanced at it. "Yeah. It's a .308 rifle shell cut to fit the .44 magnum automatic. So what about it?"

Neither of them noticed the small TV camera high up in the corner of the room swivel to take in the scene. Someone, somewhere else in the club, was watching them.

"You think you could make me some just like this?" Axel leaned on the display case.

"If I had the time. Where did you get this one?"

"It was a present from Clint Eastwood," Axel deadpanned.

Russ was not amused. "Why did you come in here? Just to break my balls? Is that it?"

Russ was getting warmed up when a woman swept into the room. She was tall, blond, and had ice-blue eyes. Axel's jaw dropped. This was one incredibly beautiful woman. Axel wondered if she would care to come home with him and be the mother of many, many of his children.

"I'm Karla Fry," she said with a toss of her great blond mane. "I'm the assistant manager here."

"Richard James," said Axel. "Congratulations, you are doing a wonderful job."

"Glad you like it. Russ? Could I see you for a minute?"

Russ lumbered out from behind the counter and Karla took him by one beefy arm and led him out into the lobby.

"I'll just wait in here," said Axel. They ignored him.

"Who is that man?" she demanded.

Fielding shrugged. "I don't know. He's got a .44-auto-mag casing from here."

"Damn," hissed Karla. "Are you sure it's one of ours?"

Russ knew his own work when he saw it. "Yeah,

I'm sure. I made that one and a whole bunch of other ones just like it for Mr. Cain."

"You didn't tell him that, did you?" she asked coldly. Panic wasn't in her repertoire of emotions.

"No."

"Don't," she ordered. "And keep him there while I check him out."

Karla crossed the lobby and went to a bank of elevators that stood against one wall. Taking a key from her pocket, she unlocked the door to a private, executive elevator and went up to the fourth floor of the clubhouse. She walked down a long hall and pushed open a set of double doors marked "Mr. Dent." She breezed through the outer office and walked boldly into Maxwell Dent's office. She was the only person in the place who had free access at any time to *the* Maxwell Dent. Everyone else had to wait to be summoned to the inner sanctum.

Dent's office was silent, frigid, austere—like the man himself. He sat behind a wide glass-and-aluminum desk on which sat nothing more than a blotter and a telephone. Behind him was a bank of TV monitors, about a dozen screens. From here he could see virtually everything that was going on in his domain. The Beverly Hills Shooting Club was owned exclusively by Dent. He turned from the monitor on which he had been watching Axel when Karla came into the room.

He fixed his gray eyes on her. "Well?"

"I think we have a problem," said Karla, tight-lipped. "Russ says he made that casing for Cain."

One of Dent's long, thin fingers snaked out and

tapped the intercom button on his phone. "Send Chip Cain in here immediately." He had a slight accent, possibly German or Scandinavian.

"One of the hired guns on the Adriano's job used a .44 auto mag," said Karla.

Dent immediately picked up the thread. "Cain had a special casing made *here* for a gun that was used on the Adriano's job. And now someone walks in here asking questions. It is unbelievably stupid, even for Cain."

Karla shrugged. Cain would serve their purposes.

"Go back to our guest," said Dent calmly, "and keep him here while I decide what to do with him."

There was a knock at the door. "Come in," snapped Dent.

Chip Cain appeared. The first impression you had of him was his smoothness. Smooth clothes, smooth skin, smooth moves. But after a while you began to realize that he was a bit of a jerk. His smoothness seemed to be a veneer over the real Chip Cain. The real Chip Cain wasn't smooth at all.

"I would like to go over the plans for C and D," said Dent in clipped, pointed syllables.

Cain looked a little surprised. "But we just went over this . . ."

Dent glanced up at him, silencing him with a look. Then he spoke slowly and carefully, as if explaining something quite simple to an unusually dim-witted child.

"We have promised to deliver to Mr. Thomopolis ten million dollars. We must do this by six P.M. tomorrow. Are you with me so far, Chip?"

Cain didn't like to be talked to this way, but Maxwell Dent was the boss, and Cain always did what he was told.

"If we fail," Dent went on in the same slow voice, "I stand to be put to considerable expense and inconvenience, to say the least. So"—he paused, making sure that he had Cain's full attention—"I would like to go over it again and possibly avoid the mistakes that were made on the Adriano's job."

"What mistakes? Adriano's was perfect."

Dent's voice was as warm as a bear trap. "Adriano's was not perfect. It was planned perfectly, but it was executed with neolithic incompetence." He rubbed his brow and his voice took on a self-pitying note. "It is partly my fault. I, for some reason, assumed that if my instructions were clear enough, even you, Chip, could follow them. Obviously, I was wrong."

Cain shook his head. "I don't understand."

Dent looked up at the soundproofed ceiling of his office, as if talking to God. "He doesn't understand."

Then he fixed an icy gaze on Chip Cain. Cain squirmed in his seat.

"Let me try to shine a light through the thick fog shrouding your pathetic little mind. You fucked up." Dent still had not raised his voice. "I have gone to a great deal of trouble to keep myself removed from these Alphabet crimes. You and Karla are the only two who know. And you supplied your thugs on the Adriano's job with guns from the club."

"Yeah," said Cain, trying to clear himself. "But

they were totally clean. They can't be traced. No-body knows you planned the jobs, you wrote the Alphabet notes. Karla did the job and left them."

Dent gripped the edge of his desk. "Then why," he demanded, "is there a man in my club with a shell casing from one of my totally clean, untraceable guns asking questions?"

Cain shrugged. "I don't know. Who is he?"

Dent was very polite. "I would say he's some kind of cop, wouldn't you?"

"I don't know, I haven't seen him."

"Well, here he is on the monitor." He tapped one of the screens. The image showed Axel with Karla on one of the shooting ranges beneath the building. Cain peered at him.

"The black guy?"

"The black guy. Now take a good look at him, Chip. Because you are going to kill him." Dent passed the death sentence on Axel in the same tone of voice that he might have used to have one of his secretaries bring him a cup of coffee.

Cain stumbled back from the monitor, as if Axel might be able to hear them. "What . . .?"

Cain shuddered to himself. He was the first to admit that he had broken a few laws but he had never killed anybody. He had always left that to others.

"You want me to—"

"Kill him, burn him, blow him away. You created the problem, now you get rid of it." He paused. "You may go."

Cain walked slowly from the room. Dent was the boss. And Cain always did what he was told. He would make sure the cop got wasted, but he was damned if he was going to pull the trigger himself.

Axel couldn't decide which he admired more—the woman or her skill with weapons. She had a five-shot Walther .22 short-match pistol in her hand—it molded to her grip perfectly—and with her arms extended down the range she shot five times, smacking the bull with each shot. Her strong arm and shoulder hardly moved on the recoil. It was as if she were cemented in place. As the sound of the last shot died in the soundproofing, she wiped the smoking barrel of the gun with a rag.

"Yes. I can shoot," she said, smirking at Axel. "Is there anything else you would like to know?"

"Now that you mention it, I'd like to know how long it takes to shave a leg as long as yours. I bet a couple of days. Next time you do it I'd like to come by—maybe bring a friend. Pack a picnic lunch . . ."

"I suppose you're trying to be charming."

"That was the idea," admitted Axel, "but I guess it didn't work."

Karla slipped the clip out of the gun and slowly started reloading it. As she did so, Chip Cain walked over as casually as if he'd just happened to be passing by.

"New member, Karla?" he asked. He was back to his old smooth self.

"Not quite, Chip. This is Chip Cain," she said. "He's the manager of the club."

Axel looked around him and nodded. "Nice place you got here. Comfortable."

Cain smiled like a proud father. "We do our best. Maybe you'd like to apply for membership."

"Absolutely," said Axel vehemently.

"Where should I send the application forms?"

"Sixteen-oh-three Hillcrest. Big white house. Can't miss it."

"Good," said Cain. "We'll get it over to you in a hurry."

Axel smiled. "Good." He glanced at his watch. "Gotta go."

"Good-bye, Mr. James."

"We'll be meeting again," Axel said, "I just know it."

Karla returned to Dent's office. He was busily crafting the next two Alphabet bandit notes.

"Chip says it's as good as done."

"I do so want to believe that," said Dent without looking up.

Karla perched on the side of his desk, her long perfect legs thrust out in front of her. "What about the cop in the hospital?"

"What about him?"

"You don't think we should try again?"

Still Dent didn't look up. "I think it is reasonably safe to assume that he will be in a coma until six P.M. tomorrow. Besides, he's guarded twenty-four hours a day. Two officers outside, one inside."

"I could take them."

Dent finished writing with a flourish. He glanced up and chuckled. "My dear Karla, this is a business venture. Not the O.K. corral."

"He didn't see you," she said bluntly.

"And he won't see you after tomorrow. There is no risk. I have planned everything perfectly." He handed her the latest note. "And here we have the next note. What it lacks in style it makes up for in content."

She glanced at the now-familiar jumble of numbers. "Will they be able to break this one?"

Dent sat back in his padded leather chair. "They will break it when we want them to."

Jack May and Willie Slotnick were the two thugs who had been on the Adriano's job and the bungled execution of Bogomil. May was the big guy with the auto mag who got his kicks shooting at things—preferably living things. Willie had grabbed the jewelry. He didn't have anything against killing either, but he liked to get paid for it. They had traded their Trans-Am for a black Camaro and were parked on a seedy side street in Hollywood. They were waiting for Cain.

May stuck a cigarette in his mouth. "Got a match?"

Willie slapped the wheel. "Where the fuck is he, man? Where the fuck is he?" Willie got nervous when he was kept waiting.

"I said, you got a match?"

"No," Willie said. "I don't smoke. You know that. Fucks you up. Your body, you know."

Jack tried to get the cigarette lighter in the car to work. It didn't. "Shit."

Willie went tense behind the wheel. "There he is."

Cain parked his Buick across the street and

walked over to the car. Willie rolled down the window and Cain thrust a wad of hundred-dollar bills in at him.

"His name is Richard James. He's black. He's a cop. Sixteen-oh-three Hillcrest." May and Willie nodded. "The man says it has to be tonight. And no screw-ups."

May leaned forward and looked up at Cain. "Yeah, yeah," he said sullenly. "Hey, you got a match?"

Cain tossed a matchbook at him.

"Can I keep these? The lighter in the car's broke." He punched it in again for effect, but it popped right out.

Cain didn't give a damn about the matches. "Jack, Willie. It's got to be tonight. And don't mess this up." Cain walked quickly away from the car. Jack May lit his cigarette, tossed the matches on top of the dash, and then leaned down and picked up a gun that was on the floor of the car. It was an MP-5K machine pistol that sprayed bullets like a hose turned on full blast. He twisted on a bulky silencer.

"Let's go," he said to Willie.

CHAPTER SEVEN

Axel rang the doorbell at Bogomil's house a couple of times and then checked the garage. No cars. Jan wasn't home yet. Well, he figured that Jan wouldn't mind if he just let himself in. He walked around the back of the modest house and popped the rear lock with a credit card. He shook his head. What was it about cops that they never had good locks on their doors?

He crossed the kitchen and made his way directly to Bogomil's office, which was connected to his bedroom by a large closet. Axel couldn't miss the file. It was red and it was sitting right on top of the desk where he had left it the morning he had been suspended—and shot.

Axel sat down and flipped through it, picking up each carefully cut-out piece of paper and trying to see how they all fit together.

He was reading about the international oil market when a voice behind him shouted: "Freeze!"

Axel whipped around, going for his gun, then stopped. It was Jan and she had a gun on him already. If he had been a burglar, she would have dropped him before he could have gotten his gun out of his belt. She went limp when she saw him.

"Not bad." Axel laughed. "Your father's daughter. I'm sorry. I just let myself in. How are you?"

Jan dropped her gun into her purse. "Tired," she said. "I knew I said I'd be here, but I went into the office to get some work to do at home. Keep my mind off things, you know."

"You still work at the, what was it, the insurance company?"

Jan nodded. "It's not exciting, but you practically never get shot at."

"That would make a nice change. Man, I think there must be more guns in this town than in all of Detroit. You've got a gun—I just spent an hour at the Beverly Hills Shooting Club. They got enough guns *there* to take over, I dunno, France or something."

"That's Beverly Hills. Did you find anything?"

"Just this," said Axel, holding up the file.

"Anything there?"

Axel shrugged. "Hard to say. There's a lot of stuff here about the international oil business. Then a picture of some guy named Dent and another guy named Thomopolis. Check this caption: 'Oil entrepreneur Maxwell Dent shrugs off business woes at a party with international munitions trader, Nicko Thomopolis.'"

"That's a coincidence," said Jan. "Dent owns the club you were just at."

Axel paused. Coincidence? He doubted it. "How do you know that?"

Jan shrugged. "Common knowledge around here, I guess."

Axel picked up a couple of papers. "Your dad was very interested in the fall of oil prices. Did he invest in oil or anything?"

Jan shook her head and laughed. "On a cop's pay? No way."

"Yeah, I know the feeling. . . ." He glanced down at the folder again. "I also found this ad. It's for a nightclub called 385 North. Know it?"

Jan shook her head again.

Axel was thinking hard. "Listen, I think he was shot because he was on to something. Was there anything unusual about where he went lately?"

Jan frowned. "No, nothing. You know Dad . . . always by the clock. And I don't think he was hanging around any nightclubs." She slumped into a chair.

Axel could see that Jan was exhausted, but he needed her help. "Hey, I know you're tired. But you could do one thing for me."

Jan looked up. "Anything, Axel."

"I want you to go into work—"

"But, Axel, they just sent me home—"

"Not today, tomorrow. Use your contacts at the insurance company to find out what you can about this guy Dent. Ask around. Pull a file. Anything will help. If you find anything, call Rosewood. He'll find me."

Jan looked dubious. "I'll try, Axel, but I don't promise anything."

"Okay." He nudged her gently. "Get some sleep. Go get some rest. And don't shoot anybody, okay?"

"I won't," she said, smiling now.

Axel took one last look around the room and decided there was nothing more to be seen there. He was about to leave when he noticed Bogomil's running shoes in the hallway that led to his bedroom.

They were covered in red mud. He looked at the running suit that was hanging in the closet. The pants were spattered with mud up to the knee.

Outside the house, Axel knelt and examined the dirt in Bogomil's yard. It was dark, almost black. Wherever that mud had come from, it hadn't come from around there. Still thinking about it, he got in behind the wheel of the Caddy and slowly drove away, filling the immaculate street with clouds of exhaust.

"He said meet him in an hour at 1603 Hillcrest," said Rosewood, behind the wheel of the green Beverly Hills Police Department Plymouth Fury.

"Yeah," grumbled Taggart, watching as the neighborhood changed gradually from classy to grand and finally to sumptuously magnificent. "That's what worries me, Billie. These aren't houses anymore; these are palaces."

"Sarge, you sound like a rube on the Stars' Homes Tour."

"Okay, I'll let *you* worry about what he's doing in this neighborhood."

But that wasn't what was on Billie's mind. He was far more involved with Taggart's marital troubles. He was trying to cheer him up.

"You know," he said sympathetically, "she knew you were hard to live with when she married you. I actually fault her for thinking you'd change."

"Thanks," growled Taggart. "Make a left down here, Billie."

Rosewood's point of view had run around to the other side of Taggart's problem and was viewing it from his wife's perspective. "Although, in a funny way I actually admire her for having the courage to leave you and search for a better life."

"Shut up, Billie," said Taggart. He stuck a black cigar in his mouth and lit it.

"And that's no good for you either," said Billie gently.

"It calms me down," said Taggart. "Makes me feel better."

Rosewood shook his head and looked chagrined. "I guess I was trying to cheer you up, but I went off on a tangent. I'll bet you're still thinking that we're out of a job and Maureen will still get a big alimony and you don't know how you can afford it, am I right?"

"Hell, Billie," said Taggart unhappily, "I'm fifty years old. I got angina. First I lost my hair and now I lost my wife. What the hell am I going to do if I lose my job?"

"I'll bet Axel could get you a job in Detroit," said Billie soothingly.

"That's wonderful, Billie, a very practical suggestion. Go from the dangerous life of a Beverly Hills policeman to the calm streets of Detroit. Take a break from cheering me up, will you?"

Rosewood stood on the brakes. "Hey, this is the place. Jesus, would you look at it!"

They stared up at the Rosenberg mansion. It looked like a cross between Tara from *Gone With the Wind* and a tastefully toned-down version of the palace at Versailles.

They got out of the car and peered through the gates. "This has *got* to be a mistake," exclaimed

Taggart. The angina pain in his arm increased dramatically. He rubbed it vigorously.

"There's his car," said Rosewood. Way up the driveway, there was the beat-up Eldorado.

Taggart was very nervous now. "Billie, if he's here, he must be robbing the place."

"We better find out." Billie swung open the gate and started up the long drive.

From a block away, Willie and Jack watched them enter the house.

"Cops," said Jack. He could always tell cops when he saw them.

The front door of the house was open and the two detectives tiptoed in, not quite able to believe what they were doing. The place was pure Beverly Hills. The newly laid carpet was a pastel pink, but still had plastic runners on it so the workmen wouldn't get it dirty. Rosewood and Taggart kept scrupulously to the little plastic highways that ran all over the house. The kitchen was as high-tech as they come—it looked like it belonged in a restaurant, not a private home. The food processor alone had more dials and buttons than the cockpit of a 747.

"Axel?" called Rosewood.

"I don't like this," said Taggart. He had broken out in a cold sweat. "What would he be doing in a place like this?"

"Maybe the Pointer Sisters live here or something."

Suddenly there was the sound of someone screaming. Both men froze. "Where the hell did that come from?" hissed Taggart.

There was another scream.

"Backyard!" said Taggart. "Let's go."

Both of them pulled out their guns and ran like hell for the terrace doors. They jumped out onto the patio, both of them in the combat stance, their guns trained on . . . Axel, sitting in a floating pool chair. He was wearing a pale green bathing suit, shades, and a big straw hat. Bogomil's files were open on his lap, but he was staring at the TV that stood at the edge of the pool. It was tuned to *Wheel of Fortune* and Axel was cheering on some guy from Providence, Rhode Island, who had guessed "garbage cans." The answer had been "garbage bags."

"You blew it man," said Axel heatedly, pointing at the set. He looked up at Taggart and Rosewood who stared in disbelief. "Hi guys, beers are in the fridge. Or I could make you a mai-tai. Oh! Forgot, you're on duty. Make that Perrier."

Billie couldn't help but laugh. "Axel, you know . . ."

Taggart saw nothing funny about it. He holstered his gun. "What the hell are you doing in a place like this?"

"I am spoiling myself rotten, Taggart. I don't mind the construction; I just confine myself to the other five bedrooms."

Taggart put his hands on his hips. "You've stolen this house, haven't you?"

"How do you steal a house, Taggart? No, this is my uncle's place. He's in Paris right now."

"Get the hell out of that pool, Axel."

"No, c'mon, strip down and take a swim. The water is great. Room temperature."

Rosewood looked hopefully at Taggart. Billie was

in the mood for a swim. And it would relax Sergeant Taggart. But Taggart wasn't having any of it. He glared back at Billie. "Forget it."

"Awww, Taggart, don't spoil the party. You can do laps. That way it'll seem like work."

Taggart had forgotten his awe of the house, of the enormous pool, of the swaying palms. He walked to the edge of the pool and squatted down almost face-to-face with Axel. "I want you out of this pool and out of this house in seven minutes," he ordered. "You're a goddamn insult to every police officer in America."

Axel leaned up. "I love it when you talk tough to me, Officer." He made a stab at giving Taggart a kiss. Taggart was taken by surprise; he recoiled and tried to stand up—but he wasn't quite steady on his feet. He started to fall backward, then overcompensated. Then, as if it had been ordained, he fell forward, his arms windmilling, into the pool.

Axel screamed with laughter and Rosewood had to duck his head and look away so Taggart couldn't see him laughing.

"I'm sure I could have found you a bathing suit if you'd asked," said Axel between cackles.

Taggart climbed out of the pool and stood there dripping and angry. "Axel, so help me—"

"No," Axel said, "no lectures, Taggart." He hopped off the floating chair and hauled himself out of the pool. "Are you boys ready to hit the town?"

Neither Rosewood nor the dripping Taggart answered.

"Okay," said Axel, "I'll answer for you. 'Yeah, Axel, where the hell we going?' Well, I'll tell you.

I'm taking you to 385 North. Now this is a classy place—I heard about it from Bogomil, believe it or not—so Taggart, go inside and try on some of my uncle's clothes. You look terrible."

It was dark when they left the house, got in the police car, and cruised down Hillcrest. Three cars behind, the black Camaro, with Willie at the wheel, followed.

Taggart felt a little better. He had never worn such nice clothes before. "Some guy over in Homicide told me that 385 North was the private club of some Greek. It's supposed to have the most beautiful women in the world," he said, almost happy.

Axel chuckled. "You love the ladies, don't you, Sarge? That's probably why Maureen split on you. Women calling you at home, stuff like that."

"Cut it, Axel."

"Hey," said Rosewood, "maybe tonight we'll find the next Mrs. Taggart." He spoke as if that was a definite possibility.

They pulled into the parking lot of 385 North. The lot alone looked to Axel like the forecourt of a foreign-auto dealer's showroom. Apart from the Plymouth, there didn't seem to be an American car anywhere in sight. There were neat rows of BMWs, Mercedeses, and Bentleys.

"Doesn't anybody in this town drive something normal, like maybe a Ford?"

"Only cops and servants," growled Taggart.

Rosewood was looking at the club itself. It was a long, low building with no windows showing out to the street. Periodically, though, the large red door would swing open and some members would come stumbling out, a gust of loud music following them. A tuxedoed figure stood at the front door. He was 385 North's version of Raul. Above his bulky shoulder was a small brass plate. On it were some of Axel's favorite words: "Members Only."

"How you going to get around that, Axel?" asked Rosewood.

"I'm going to take out my gun and badge and announce that we are raiding the establishment."

Taggart felt a sharp pain in his chest. "Axel!" he barked.

Rosewood rolled his eyes. "He's just kidding, Sarge." Then he looked at Axel. "You *are* kidding, aren't you?"

Axel was looking at the bouncer. "Yeah. I'm just kidding." They all got out of the car. "You two wait here," he said. "Taggart, try not to stand in the light too much."

"Why the hell not?"

"Because you are about to become famous."

Axel strode up to the door and started to walk in. A hand caught him by the shoulder and pulled him back. "Excuse me, sir, are you a member?" Close up, the guy looked very big and the grip he had on Axel's shoulder spoke volumes about his strength.

"No," said Axel, "I'm not. I was just going in to check on security."

The man looked puzzled. "Security? Pal, you are looking at the security. I'm it. Happy? Now this is a private club, so . . ."

Axel shook his head and smiled. "I'm sorry, I'm

sorry, this is my fault. I guess the service screwed up. You were supposed to be notified."

"Notified? Notified of what?"

Axel swung around and pointed at Taggart. "Do you realize who that is?"

The bouncer looked at Taggart. He did not seem to register instant comprehension.

Axel laughed. "That's right. That man with the receding hairline"—he dropped his voice to a whisper—"is ex-President Gerald Ford."

Taggart caught the tuxedoed man staring at him. He couldn't hear what they were saying but he smiled back. The bouncer smiled.

"He doesn't look like Gerald Ford," said the doorman dubiously.

"Oh, yeah, and you see a lot of Gerald Ford, right?" Axel paused while the man continued to peer at Taggart.

"See," Axel explained, "when you're president you can't go to shit like this. But he loves his shimmy dancing more than golf."

The bouncer still wasn't convinced. "Well, if that's Gerald Ford, who are you?

Axel grinned and hauled out his badge. "Axel Foley, Secret Service. You think the man just walks around like he was a nobody?"

Taggart saw Axel flash his badge. "Oh, shit, Billie, he just showed his badge."

"Oh, no, of course not," the bouncer said. He was also thinking what the Greek would do to him if it got in the gossip columns that Gerald Ford had been turned away from 385 North by an officious flunky.

"It's a pleasure to have him here, Mr. Foley. I'll see that he gets an excellent table. I'm sorry about the delay. You can't be too careful."

"The president appreciates that." Axel walked back to Taggart and Rosewood. "We're in, boys."

"We *are?*" said Taggart in disbelief.

"Yup." Axel led them toward the door and the bouncer opened it ceremoniously for him. "I voted for you, sir," he said as Taggart passed.

"What the hell does that mean?" hissed Taggart.

"He thinks you're Gerald Ford. Act presidential."

Taggart felt the pain in his chest tighten a notch. The interior of 385 North was low-lit. In designer terms, the decor was sort of Moorish-Roman —it was as if someone had crossed the Colosseum with the Casbah. There were thick Persian carpets on the floor, marble on the walls, and lights and lasers that spotlit the dance floor and the stage on which a stripper was just concluding her act. To make the place more "intimate," there there were candles on the low tables. The place was packed and the music was loud and everyone— particularly Axel—seemed to be having a good a good time.

Even Taggart relaxed a little. The place *did* have the most beautiful women he had ever seen. As he looked from table to table or over at the waitresses who were getting drink orders from a service bar, he saw nothing but dynamite women. He felt his mouth go dry.

A waitress came over to their table. She was wearing a skirt so short it appeared to be a wide belt, and her low-cut blouse covered most of her breasts rather more by accident than design. As she leaned over the table, Rosewood's Adam's apple started going up and down like an elevator.

"What can I get you gentlemen?" she purred.

She smiled demurely at Taggart. She'd always thought that Gerald Ford was older than that, but that only proved how TV aged you. Then she glanced at Rosewood and caught him looking directly at her cleavage. His order was written all over his face. She smiled at him. "You can have anything but that, honey," she said, smiling and straightening to avoid his gaze. Rosewood turned the color of a freshly boiled lobster.

"I'll have a scotch and water. Mr. President will have a club soda and my colleague here will have the same."

"With a twist," said Rosewood suavely.

Axel wasn't looking at the stripper anymore, or even at the act that replaced her. He watched as three obvious bodyguard types took up positions near the men's room. A few seconds later a tall, powerfully built man with a mustache that looked like the business end of a pushbroom came out. The goons almost genuflected when he appeared. They fell in next to their boss and headed for the exit.

Axel got up from the table and ambled over to the bar. The bartender's back was turned to him. "Hey," he said, "quick, who was that guy with the big ugly mustache. Looks like he's got a squirrel on his face?"

The bartender turned around. He wore an identical mustache. "Nikos Thomopolis," he said, surly, "he owns this place."

Axel stared at the guy's upper lip, or where his upper lip should have been. How was he supposed to know that there would be two mustaches like that in one place. "Nice tie," he said, and went back to the table.

Taggart had gotten off to a bad start with the stripper. "My name is John Taggart," he said before he remembered.

Axel returned. "The name Thomopolis mean anything to you?"

"He's the biggest arms dealer on the West Coast."

Axel looked back at the door. "C'mon," he said, "let's go."

As they walked to the door, the little Mediterranean band swung into "Hail to the Chief," a lot of it played on the mandolin. Drinkers and dancers muttered their confusion at the change of tune. Several swiveled and craned their necks to try and identify the celebrity.

Outside the club a crowd of people had gathered. Some were leaving and were waiting for the parking valets to find their Mercedeses; others were just arriving.

"Gerald Ford is a lot older than I am," grumbled Taggart. "Do I really look like Gerald Ford?"

"Yeah," said Rosewood, "kinda. When you're rested."

Axel was looking for Thomopolis. He scanned the lot and down the drive that led up to the club entrance. A car was coming toward him. It was the Camaro. "Hey, look, an American car. Made in

103

Deee—" Suddenly the Camaro speeded up, the tires peeling, the engine screaming. The car came racing toward the club, slamming to a stop parallel with the entrance.

Axel spread his arms wide and screamed: "Get down!" He threw himself into the crowd of people, as if he were trying to tackle the entire front line of the Dallas Cowboys. He knocked a half-dozen expensively dressed men and women flat to the ground as the first deadly bullets from Jack May's machine pistol splattered against the facade of the building.

Lead was flying everywhere. Women were screaming and everybody was diving for cover. The MP-5K was blasting nine steel-jacketed rounds a second, gouging great gouts of concrete out of the forecourt and the building itself.

Axel dove behind a Mercedes. May caught the movement and he swung his gun toward Axel, his trail of lead following closely, missing him by inches. The Mercedes took the worst of it. The windows splashed open and the tires exploded with a noise like a pistol shot.

Abruptly, the firestorm stopped. May yanked out the spent magazine and scrambled to get a new one in. Axel took full advantage of the lull. He jumped up from behind the Mercedes, coming up firing. The 9mm bullets tore into the Camaro. The windshield disappeared in a shower of glass chips. Axel pumped off round after round. Slugs slammed into the door paneling, shredding leather and tearing iron.

Willie started losing it. He hadn't expected returning fire. This was supposed to be a clean job. Willie decided it was time to get the hell out of there. Just as May got the machine pistol working again, hurling a couple of tons of lead in a fiery orange arc across the shattered Mercedes, Willie tried to slam the car in gear, but succeeded in simply popping the clutch. The car lurched forward and threw Jack back in his seat, causing May to fire wildly, missing the Mercedes completely.

"Son of a bitch," screamed May, "what the fuck are you doing?"

"Getting outta here!"

As the Camaro roared toward the street, Axel jumped from his cover and unloaded a fresh clip of 9mm bullets into the tail of the black car. The rear window shattered. A few well-placed shots shredded the rear tires. Willie lost control of the car just about the same time he lost his mind. The speeding Camaro sideswiped a Bentley Mulsanne, bounced off, crushed a Jaguar, and jumped the curb, careening from the parking lot to disappear around a corner. A second after it disappeared, there was the sound of a crash as Willie gave up trying to drive his mortally wounded automobile.

Axel leaped to his feet. He shouted over his shoulder: "Taggart! Get a goddamn ambulance!"

Revenge was very much on Axel's mind as he raced after the Camaro. He was prepared to bet the rest of his life's salary that those two had had something to do with the hit on Bogomil. Also, Axel deeply resented being shot at—it annoyed him.

The Camaro was wrapped around a light pole, both doors were open, and there was no sign of the two gunmen. Axel stopped running, his gun hand dropping to his side. He slammed down hard on the roof of the trashed Camaro. "Shit."

Within ten minutes, it seemed as if two-thirds of the Beverly Hills Police Force was on the scene at 385 North. A complement of uniformed cops had quickly sealed off the crime scene. From behind sawhorses bystanders gawked at the police, the written-off Camaro, the bullet-riddled facade of the exclusive club. Axel leaned against the fender of a police black-and-white, watching Jim Williams, a self-important member of the forensics wing of the B.H.P.D. removing evidence and placing it in the bags.

Axel walked over to the car, and picked up the book of matches that May had tossed on top of the dash. He picked it up and held it out to Williams.

"Want to check this for prints?"

Williams was condescending. "Look, pal, will you just back away from the car? You're interfering with my job." He looked scornfully at Axel. "Any idiot knows you can't get prints off a matchbook."

Axel shrugged. "Anything you say, Professor Wizard."

He walked away, carefully wrapping the match-book in a handkerchief. He slid it into his pocket. He walked over to Taggart and Rosewood. They were talking to a couple of uniforms.

Taggart still couldn't believe what had happened. "When we got here," he explained to the uniforms, "the car was empty. Whoever it was got away clean." He shook his head in wonderment.

"It's crazy," said Rosewood. "They must have fired a hundred rounds, but didn't hit anyone. One lady was hurt, but that was from flying glass."

"Uh-oh," said Taggart. A car came careening into the lot and stopped with a screech of brakes. It was Lutz and, of course, Biddle.

Lutz made a beeline for Taggart, Rosewood, and Axel. The two uniformed officers suddenly found something else to do and faded away.

"You! James!" roared Lutz. "I checked with the federal marshal's office and they never heard of you. I want to know who the hell you are, and what the hell is going on. And I want to know *now*." His yells echoed around the lot, drowning out the radio chatter coming from the police units and temporarily silencing the mumbling bystanders.

Axel pulled out his Detroit badge and sighed. "Okay," he said, as though resigned. "I'm Detective Axel Foley. I didn't tell you before because I knew it would upset you. And I didn't want to cause you any problems."

Lutz grabbed the badge and stared at it. "A cop? *You?* A cop?"

Axel nodded. "That's right."

Williams, the prints man, came over. "No prints in the car, Chief. The car was reported stolen two hours ago."

"Thanks, Williams," said Lutz dismissively. He turned back to Axel. "That's a Detroit badge. What the hell are you doing in Beverly Hills?"

The lie came out smooth as silk. "I'm attached to a multijurisdictional federal task force on organized crime."

Rosewood and Taggart did their level best not to look surprised. Lutz turned a deeper shade of red.

"I'm the goddamn chief of police. If there's some federal task force here, I want to know about it."

Axel shook his head. "See, I knew you'd be upset."

"Upset isn't the word, pal."

Axel's voice was cold and commanding. "My assignment is top secret. I can't talk to anybody about it."

"You can talk to me. At least, you *better* talk to me about it or . . ."

"Sorry, Chief Lutz. I can't. You have no jurisdiction in this."

"You watch your mouth, Foley."

"Look," said Axel, trying to be conciliatory, "my commanding officer in Detroit is Inspector Todd. You can call the Detroit P.D. and he'll verify this assignment. He'll be in his office in the morning, between nine and ten, Detroit time. I'm sorry, that's all I can tell you."

Lutz was steaming mad. "I'll call him," he stormed, "goddamn right I'll call him."

"Good. That should clear everything up." Axel walked away, as if there were nothing more to say.

Lutz turned the full force of his fury on Rosewood and Taggart. "And I suppose *you* just happened to be in the area checking parking meters, right?"

"Well, sir . . ." began Taggart. When confronted, Taggart, despite his desire to keep his job, had an alarming tendency to tell the truth. Rosewood was not going to have that happen. After all, he had learned *something* from Axel.

"We were just going off duty, sir," said Billie, "when we heard a call that all units in this area should roll." Rosewood shrugged. "We rolled."

Lutz wanted to bite something. He had personally given the order for the movement of all units in the area of 385 North. "If I see you two anywhere except traffic duty, I'll have you investigated and fired. Got it?"

To Taggart and Rosewood, it came through loud and clear.

CHAPTER
EIGHT

Mozart's Concerto for Flute and Harp was playing softly in Billie Rosewood's small apartment. As Axel followed Rosewood and Taggart into the apartment, he had only one thing on his mind. "Billie, you are sure you got super glue?"

"Yes, Axel, I'm sure."

Axel walked straight into the small living room and looked around him. There were plants everywhere. Hanging in the window, lining the windowsills, spilling out of planters on the floor. It was like living outside.

"Billie," exclaimed Axel, "this is the wild kingdom."

Taggart didn't like plants. He tried to avoid touching them, although it was difficult to keep away from them in Billie's indoor garden.

"These are my friends, Axel." Billie touched a feathery Boston fern. "This is Mona." Lovingly, he touched another. "This is a Charlie, he's a Wandering Jew. This is Marcel, a Dieffenbachia. And here's Ben, the Ficus benjamina."

Axel watched Rosewood carefully; he was sure that Billie was turning into a raving lunatic right before his eyes. But Billie was sincere, lost in the complicated introductions. "And by the window is Elaine, Bobby, and little Max. The Bromeliads."

"I guess it was Marcel who turned on the stereo," said Axel.

"No," said Billie seriously, "I did. It's always on. They actually like different kinds of music. The begonias thrive on the Beatles, but if you play Beethoven they wither. The ferns adore the Boston Pops. But they all agree on Mozart."

As Billie turned the stereo down, Axel crouched to examine a terrarium that was home to a turtle.

"That's Big Al," said Billie.

"Lemme guess, he likes James Brown."

"I've had him six years. Isn't he something?"

"Obviously a thoroughbred," said Axel. Unceremoniously, Axel removed the top of Big Al's terrarium, reached in, and pulled out Big Al. He set him with a plop on the floor.

"Giving Big Al a chance to stretch his legs. Where's the super glue?"

Rosewood scooped up the turtle and gently carried him away. Taggart, who had watched all this in silence, finally spoke. "You think Billie might be from another planet, Axel?"

"Either that or his parents were elves."

Rosewood returned with a tube of glue. "Great," said Axel. He took the tube from Billie, ripped the top off the container, and put it in the terrarium. Axel then reached into his pocket, took out the handkerchief, and carefully removed the matchbook. He placed it in the terrarium close to the oozing glue.

"That stuff is going to ruin the environment of the habitat," Rosewood said nervously.

"You can apply to the EPA for a cleanup grant," said Axel. "Where's the phone, Billie? In the alligator pit?"

He pointed down the hall. "In the bedroom."

There were more plants in the bedroom, but they weren't the only decoration. On the walls were posters of "Dirty Harry" and "Cobra." The room looked like a shrine to Dirty Harry.

On the bed was giant stuffed pink pig wearing a policeman's uniform. Axel rubbed his eyes and smiled. "Jesus, Billie."

He sat down on the edge of the bed and dialed a number. He waited a long time before his call was answered.

"Jeffrey, it's Axel. Yeah, yeah, yeah. I know what time it is in Detroit."

Jeffrey had been sound asleep, but he immediately got his mouth cranked up and started babbling. Axel listened for a minute.

"Beverly did what? In the Ferrari? With the *gearshift?*" Axel slapped his forehead. He had created a monster. "Jeffrey, stop talking for a minute. You've got to do something for me. You aren't going to want to," he warned, "but you gotta do it."

Jeffrey started talking again.

"I don't want to hear it, Jeffrey. You listen to me. You have the goddamn car because I gave it to you, and because of that you got Beverly. And if you want to keep them for a while, you have to do what I say. Now listen . . ."

Taggart had been persuaded to take a seat, sitting uncomfortably between an enormous spider plant and a grape ivy. He watched the sprawling plants warily, as if expecting one or the other to put out a tentacle and strangle him.

Axel reappeared and went straight to the terrarium. "There will be a call to Detroit on your phone bill, Billie. Put it on my tab, okay?" Axel glanced down at the terrarium and smiled at Taggart and Rosewood. "It worked," he said.

The two detectives stared at the matchbook cover. A fully formed thumbprint stood out on the cardboard where there had been just paper before.

"How the hell did that happen?" asked Taggart.

"See what happens is, the fumes from the super glue attach to the acid on the fingerprints. It's an old street-cop trick. Hasn't filtered down to geniuses like Professor Wizard yet."

Axel took the matchbook out of the glass case. He grinned. "Now all we gotta do is match it."

Rosewood looked at Taggart and Taggart looked back at Rosewood.

"Well, we could use the computer at headquarters," said Rosewood slowly. Taggart shook his head vigorously. But Axel nodded and grinned.

"There wouldn't be anyone there at this hour," continued Rosewood.

"There wouldn't be anyone there at this hour," echoed Axel.

Taggart seemed to sag. "There goes my medical insurance," he said, resigned.

There wasn't a soul in the computer room at headquarters. Rosewood swung into action. He slid the print into the laser computer, fingerprint ID system. He sat down at a computer keyboard, faced the monitor, and typed some instructions into the machine.

"Jesus, you guys are high-tech," said Axel with frank admiration. "It would take a million cops sixty years to do that in Detroit."

The machine silently considered the problem it had been presented with. In a matter of seconds, the machine connected to the state fingerprint bank at the state capital—Sacramento—hit a match. A rap sheet kicked out into a tray.

Axel picked it up. There was a name, a description, driver's license number, a string of prior convictions, and the last known address and place of employment. There was even a dot-matrix picture of the suspect. Axel smiled as he looked at the image.

"Hey," said Axel delightedly, "I know this guy."

Rosewood peered over Axel's shoulder. "Who is he?"

"He's the manager of the Beverly Hills Shooting Club."

"What's it say?" asked Taggart.

"Says his name used to be Charles Campos. Didn't like his old name, so he changed to Charles 'Chip' Cain."

"No law against that."

Axel studied the computer printout. "This surprises me. I mean, Cain struck me as a weasel sort of guy. Not a master criminal."

"That's his print. The machine doesn't lie."

"Yeah, I know that, but this *can't* be why Bogomil got shot. If Andrew suspected this guy, he could have picked him up with a pair of tweezers." He looked up at Rosewood and Taggart. "There's still not a whole puzzle here, guys."

"We could pick up Cain," said Billie, "find out what he knows."

"Are you crazy? Let them know that we're close? We've got one goddamn fingerprint. We can't prove he was even in the car. We need more and I don't have much time."

"So what are we going to do?" asked Rosewood, perplexed.

Axel got an odd look on his face, and his eyes lit up strangely. Involuntarily, Taggart shuddered. Whatever it was Axel was thinking, he was sure he wasn't going to like it.

"It's goblin time!" Axel said, leaning back and cracking a wide grin.

They parked in the quiet street in front of the gates of the Beverly Hills Shooting Club. It was getting on for two o'clock in the morning and the street was deserted. No light showed from the palatial club.

"No guard," observed Taggart. "No watchman. But there's gotta be security."

"There is," said Axel. He opened the door and stood beside the car in the cool night air. Nonchalantly, he pulled two sticks of gum from his pocket, stripped off the tinfoil wrappers, and thrust the gum into his mouth. He stuck the wrappers back in his pants pocket. Rosewood and Taggart joined him on the curb.

"Are you going in there, Axel?" demanded Taggart.

Axel was still looking up at the gun club building. "Uh-huh."

"That's breaking the law," hissed Taggart. "Once you step onto that property, there's no way back. It's a crime."

"And what was shooting Andrew? A misdemeanor?"

Calmly, Rosewood said, "I'll go." Secretly he was excited by the whole idea.

The remark about Bogomil had hit home. "The hell with it," said Taggart. "We'll all go."

Axel nudged Taggart and pointed at the roof. In the shadows he could make out the curve of a micro-electronic dish. "What's that?"

"*That's* the security," said Axel. "It means that this is one very well-protected building. No need for guards."

"Great," said Taggart.

"There is one thing we need, Taggart, before we commit this crime."

"Yeah, a brilliant attorney."

"No," said Axel, "a cigar. You got a cigar?"

"I didn't know you smoked cigars, Axel," said Billie.

"Yeah," said Taggart, "I got a whole box full."

"Good," said Axel, finally taking his eyes off the dish on the roof. "Then let's get going."

They climbed over the low fence, dropping noiselessly to the ground, their falls cushioned by the soft, luxuriant lawn that surrounded the clubhouse. Quickly, they made their way around the building away from the side that fronted onto the street. Axel stopped at a ground-floor window and sat himself on the sill. He took a flashlight from Billie and looked at the half-moon lock that secured the lower half of the window.

"There's alarm tape on all the glass," whispered Taggart.

"I see it," said Axel. He slipped a pocketknife open and worked the thin blade in between the two halves of the window. He tapped the lock lightly four or five times, working the rounded edge into an open position. Rosewood watched with the same awe he had trained on the waitress at 385 North earlier that night.

"How the hell did you do that?" asked Taggart.

"I wasn't born a cop, Taggart. I fractured a law once in a while when I was a kid."

Rosewood grinned. "This is fun."

"You know," said Axel, "this *is* fun." He pulled the two silver gum wrappers out of his pocket, laid the tinfoil on the flat side of the knife blade, and worked it along the crack in the window.

"What the hell are you doing now?" demanded Taggart.

"This alarm tape is connected inside by two magnets," said Axel as if he were teaching a college-level course in breaking and entering. He continued to slide the knife along the window frame as he spoke. "If we were to open the window now, we'd break the connection and the alarm would go off." He worked the knife and the tinfoil a little farther along. "So what we got to do is fool these magnets into thinking that they are still connected to one another." He jammed the tinfoil in between the two magnets and slowly raised the window an inch or two. The gum wrappers dangled from one of the magnets. He took the gum out of his mouth and, reaching in, stuck the tinfoil in place. Then he pushed the window up all the way, turned to Rosewood and Taggart, and grinned widely. "No applause please, gentlemen, I was just doing my job."

Rosewood grinned back and started to crawl through the open window. Quickly Axel caught him by the arm. "Not so fast, Billie."

Axel pointed to the corner of the room. A tiny red dot glowed in the darkness.

"There's a whole grid of laser beams crossing this room. We break one and the alarm goes off. Taggart, get out your cigar."

Taggart pulled one of his long stogies from a breast pocket and stuck it in his mouth. Axel lit it for him.

"Now, start puffing. Blow as much smoke into that room as you can."

Taggart's lungs inflated and the tip of the cigar grew red and hot as he puffed great mouthfuls of smoke into the room. Very slowly, the smoke settled to the floor, illuminating a set of bluish beams of light that ran as straight and regular across the room as railway tracks.

Taggart pulled the cigar out of his mouth. And grabbed his arm. "Oh shit . . . my heart can't stand this, Foley."

"Oh my God," breathed Rosewood. "I would have walked right in there."

"Now we go in. But don't step on any of those

beams or we'll be up to our tits in trouble. Taggart, you go first. And keep puffing that cigar."

With Taggart leading the way, like a larger version of the little engine that could, they made their way carefully down a hallway. Axel remembered Karla Fry taking an elevator—he assumed the managerial offices were on the second floor. With Taggart still puffing, they tiptoed through the picket fences of blue beams up a flight of stairs and stopped in front of an office door marked "Mr. Cain." Axel tried the handle. It was locked. In a matter of seconds he worked it open with a credit card.

Axel peered around the door but didn't see a laser projector in any of the four corners of the room. They slipped inside and closed the door. "You can stop smoking that thing now, Taggart."

Taggart took the cigar out of his mouth and breathed deeply. "I have never enjoyed a cigar less," he said.

"Just wait for the return trip."

Rosewood was shining his flashlight around the office. "Just what are we looking for?"

"Needle in a haystack, I'm afraid, Billie."

They opened the filing cabinets and found membership lists for the club, lists of dues paid, dues owed. There were sheafs of material on guns and equipment the club had ordered. Nothing they wouldn't have expected to find in the office of the manager of a gun club.

Axel sat down behind Cain's desk and opened drawers at random. They revealed average desk equipment: pens, papers, files. One drawer, however, was locked.

"Hey," he said, "give me a little light over here." Rosewood shone the flashlight beam on the desk. Axel took out his pocketknife and tried to jimmy open the lock. All he succeeded in doing was snapping the blade in two pieces. "Shit," he whispered, and looked at the top of the desk for a letter opener or some other implement.

Then, with surprising sureness, Rosewood reached into his pocket and pulled out a switchblade that looked as long as a machete and as narrow as a stiletto.

Just when Taggart thought he had seen the final depths of Billie's weirdness, his partner surprised him. When Rosewood pulled the illegal weapon out of his pocket, Taggart gasped. "Where the hell did you get that?"

"Mexico," said Rosewood. "I use it for protection on the streets."

"Hell yes," said Axel, taking the blade from Billie. "Haven't you seen those savage knife fights people get into on Rodeo Drive, Taggart?"

With Billie's weapon, Axel had the drawer open in seconds. Inside were some more letters, more club business, but there was also a yellow legal pad. Scribbled on the pad was a cryptic message:

LAT. 34 Degrees 21 Min. 510 West
LONG. 118 Degrees 3 Min.
9–10—10:30 hrs.
1 A. Car—1 Brn. Van 4—Min.

They stared at the piece of paper. "It looks like where he parked his yacht," said Taggart.

"Yeah," said Axel sarcastically, "so he can drive out to it in a car and a van. But I do have the feeling this may be the needle we have been looking for."

Axel ripped the page from the legal pad, folded the piece of paper and stowed it in his back pocket.

"We're getting close to having probable cause here on Cain. We're going to have to make a move pretty soon, Axel," said Taggart tentatively.

"Then let's get out of here," said Taggart.

"Good idea. Get your cigar going."

When the cleaners let themselves into the Beverly Hills Shooting Club the next morning, they weren't surprised to find cigar ash all over the upstairs and downstairs hall carpets. These rich people never thought of using an ashtray.

CHAPTER
NINE

It had been four A.M. Detroit time when Axel had called Jeffrey. He had been sound asleep, but now he was wide-awake. He looked out the window of his apartment at the dark city streets. "Well," he said, stretching, "this might be a good time to go for a little drive. . . ."

By seven A.M., Jeffrey had hit every after-hours club he knew and had picked up two blondes who showed him a couple of clubs he had never heard of. It had been another wild, fun-filled Ferrari night, and Jeffrey was beginning to hope that his old pal Axel would never return.

The Ferrari squealed to a halt next to a phone booth. Jeffrey checked his watch. Seven o'clock. He hadn't forgotten Axel's instructions. Now was the time. He got out of the car and staggered into the phone booth. He dialed the number and waited, winking at the girls and blowing kisses at them.

His call was answered. And Jeffrey did his best to disguise his voice: he spoke lower and slower and prayed that Todd wouldn't recognize him.

"Yes, is that Inspector Todd of the Detroit Police Department?" Todd said that it was. "Sorry to disturb you at home, Inspector. I'm—" For a second Jeffrey panicked—who was he? He knew his title,

Axel had given him that, but he didn't have a name. He stared out at the street. The first thing he saw was a toy shop with a large display of electric trains in the window. "Lionel," said Jeffrey, finally.

"Lionel who?" demanded Todd. He had had only one cup of coffee and he was standing in the hallway of his house, wrapped in a towel, dripping wet from the shower.

Jeffrey glanced down and all he saw was his hand. "Hand," he said, "Lionel Hand. I'm with the *FBI Enforcement Bulletin*. Perhaps you know the publication." Todd said he knew the *Bulletin* and that it was a fine piece of work. But he was thinking murderous thoughts about this Lionel Hand. Only a fed would call at home at seven o'clock.

"Anyway," Jeffrey continued, "the director has asked me to interview an exceptional local law enforcement officer and your name came up."

"It did?" said Todd, surprised. He knew he was a good cop but he never credited anyone else in the division with recognizing it.

"I realize it's short notice," said Jeffrey briskly, "but I was wondering if you might meet me this morning for breakfast in my office, say nine at the Federal Building." Todd said he would be glad to. He even sounded excited.

Jeffrey exhaled heavily and slumped against the side of the phone booth.

"Where we going now, Jeffie?" cooed one of the blondes.

"To work," said Jeffrey, with a sinking feeling in his stomach.

* * *

In order for Lutz to call Todd in Detroit between nine and ten Detroit time, he had had to get up earlier than usual. He was grumpy about it, but he was going to find out just what the hell a Detroit cop was doing working in his district. He wasn't ready to make the call quite yet. First he wanted some coffee and he wanted a donut; he figured he could guess what kind of answer he'd get from Detroit. . . . He would take his time.

Jeffrey wished he wouldn't. He had gotten Todd out of the office for half an hour at most. It wasn't going to take Todd long to realize that there was no Lionel Hand over at the Federal Building and Jeffrey, knowing Todd as he did, knew that the inspector would come zooming back to his office looking for somebody's blood.

Jeffrey peeked into Todd's office and was relieved to find it empty. He stepped inside and "accidentally" knocked over a stack of papers that had been tossed on top of a radiator. He crouched down and very, very slowly, began gathering them up. He stared at the phone, willing it to ring. But it didn't.

By 9:20 Jeffrey was really beginning to sweat. He was cleaning Todd's ashtrays now and picking little bits of dust up off the floor. Anything to look busy.

"Please ring," he begged the phone. Then he heard a sound that chilled him. The door of the squad room flew open and Todd's voice roared: "What rat hole son-of-a-bitch pulled my leg!"

Time to go, thought Jeffrey. Good-bye, Axel, we had a lot of fun together . . . Good-bye, Ferrari . . . Bye, girls . . . He was halfway out the door when the phone finally rang. Jeffrey dove for it and crouched down next to Todd's desk.

"Todd," he barked, as quietly as possible, into the phone.

"Inspector Todd?" asked Lutz.

"That's what I said, isn't it?" said Jeffrey gruffly.

"This is Harold Lutz," said Lutz, slightly taken aback, "chief of the Beverly Hills Police Department."

"Yeah so?" said Jeffrey. He was enjoying being Todd.

"Do you have an officer working in your command named Axel Foley?"

"Yeah, is he dead?"

"No," said Lutz, thinking that he ought to be.

"Too bad," said Jeffrey, and then he began his spiel, talking faster and faster as he went. "Yeah, he's in my command. But now he's assigned to some goddamn multijurisdictional federal task force on organized crime. I never know where the hell he is or what the hell he's doing. It's a real pain in the ass for me. I can't control the son-of-a-bitch. He reports directly to the feds. Good-bye." Jeffrey tossed the phone back into its cradle and stayed in his crouch. Todd was standing in the doorway. Jeffrey could *feel* him standing there.

"What the hell are you doing!" demanded Todd.

Jeffrey's eyes were riveted to the floorboards. "I thought I saw a rat get into your office."

"Friedman, get the hell out of here."

In the reference section of the Beverly Hills Police headquarters, a room that looked more like a college library than anything else, Axel sat at a photolight box on which were displayed sectional maps of the city. He kept glancing over at the paper he had stolen from Cain's office, trying to fit the latitude and longitude to masses of streets on the map.

"We have to figure out where these coordinates intersect."

"What makes you think they mean anything?" asked Rosewood.

"Use your head, Billie. Look, the first thing I do when I get to town is go up to that club and ask some questions. *Then* somebody tries to blow my head off. Then we find Cain's print in the car and that leads us to these coordinates."

"So you think Cain's the Alphabet bandit?"

"Starting to look that way," Axel said, peering intently at the light box. "I certainly want to be at the next robbery and see who shows up." The coordinates finally kicked into a match with a map.

"Three-forty-one Gregory Way mean anything to you guys?"

Rosewood gasped. "That's Cal Deposit."

"Cal Deposit?"

"It's a federal reserve bank. That's where banks bank their money."

"That's the next hit. I'm telling you. And I *know* what a federal reserve bank is."

"Nobody can rob that place," said Taggart firmly. "It's impregnable."

Axel looked at the paper, then up at the clock on the wall. It was 10:22. He jumped up. "Is today the twelfth?"

"Yeah," said Rosewood.

"Well, if there's going to be a robbery at Cal Deposit, we've got five minutes to stop it. Let's go."

Cal Deposit was a squat, single-story reinforced cement bunker that sat in the middle of a huge asphalt parking lot. It faced no other building, thus making it impossible to approach the ugly, secure structure without being seen. The whole building and the trucks that served it had been designed, naturally enough, with security in mind. It wasn't just Taggart who thought the building impregnable —the entire criminal population of southern California thought so too. So, despite the tens of millions of dollars—nice, old untraceable dollars—that flowed into Cal Deposit every day, no one had ever tried to rob it. Until today.

It was just about time for the midmorning delivery, and trucks from all over greater L.A. would be converging on that spot, pumping millions of dollars into the building, which was, in effect, a giant safe.

A Cal Deposit driver, a burly tattooed guy named Mendoza—he looked as if he should be out stealing money, rather than protecting it—pulled his truck up in front of the double steel doors that were the main entrance to the vaults. On the dashboard of the high-tech money wagon was a digital display and set of numbered buttons, like those on a touch-tone phone. Each truck had its own entry code and Mendoza punched his into the display on the dash. This was transmitted to the computer that controlled the doors. Instantly, the six-inch-thick steel doors started to slide open. Mendoza put his big truck in gear and drove into the unloading area of Cal Deposit, backing his truck into a numbered bay.

He climbed down from the cab and beat on the side of the truck with his billy club, letting his partner in the back know they were in, home safe and sound. The rear doors of the truck opened up and Bobby, Mendoza's partner, climbed out to stand on the loading dock. He peered through a huge bullet-proof window looking into the counting room. Inside were a dozen people in leather aprons opening heavy-duty plastic bags, dumping money on stainless-steel tables and counting it.

Mendoza went to the bullet-proof door of the counting room and punched a number into the digitally controlled lock. Like magic, the door popped open. Behind, Bobby Mendoza stood with the first of many sacks of money he had to unload.

A couple of bored, armed rent-a-cops stood around the counting room watching the cascades of money. They didn't really have much to do—after all, who would be dumb enough to try and pull something at Cal Deposit?

Outside, another truck rolled into the giant parking lot surrounding the bank. But this armored car didn't drive up to the gates. Instead, it pulled alongside the reinforced concrete wall, as if it had dropped its load of money and was parking outside before being dispatched for the afternoon pickup. Two doors opened in the side of the truck facing the wall, and Karla, in a black jumpsuit, a .357 holstered on her hip, jumped out onto the blacktop. She pulled a ski mask over her face. She was followed by an identically dressed man. He pulled what appeared to be a large metal hula-hoop out of the armored car and, with Karla's help, lugged the heavy steel ring to the wall. A third man, also in black, clambered out of the truck and the three of them hoisted the device up against the wall and secured it there with heavy, steel-threaded tape.

Just then, a brown van glided into position at the end of the armored car. Karla and her gang could not now be seen from the street. The driver of the van pulled a ski mask over his face and sat behind the wheel nervously tapping his fingers against the rim. He looked out at the traffic passing peacefully on Gregory Way, but he was alert to anything that looked even remotely like a police car.

Karla ran a series of wires from the hoop on the wall back to a detonating box. When she pressed the button, the ring of metal would heat instantly and then detonate, blasting a hole in through the concrete wall. From outside, the detonation would be no louder than someone popping an inflated paper bag. Inside the building it would be deafening.

After attaching the wires, she nodded at her companions. They stuffed ear plugs inside their ski masks and stood back from the wall. Flexing her fingers like a safecracker, Karla knelt by the box.

Inside, Bobby was lugging another heavy bag of money into the counting room.

"You better hurry up, man," wisecracked Mendoza, "or the Alphabet bandit's gonna getcha."

Bobby pointed at the wall. "How's he gonna do that, Mendoza? He gonna come right through three fucking feet of concrete wall?"

Just then, the wall exploded. What sounded like thunder rolled around the room and a white-hot hole appeared at precisely the point Bobby had been pointing to. As the wall blew in, Bobby, Mendoza, and everybody else hit the floor. Chunks of concrete flew through the air, bouncing off the side of the armored car and the bullet-proof window of the counting room.

Mendoza couldn't believe his eyes. He looked at the hole, while its bright white light—sunshine from outside—poured into the dimly lit room. The area was so choked with dust from the explosion it seemed as if they had all been swept up in an Oklahoma dust storm.

Three figures came climbing through the hole, dressed in black. They looked like alien beings as they hauled themselves into the chaos. One of them threw something and it detonated with an incredible boom. Mendoza knew he was dead. But he wasn't. He was stunned and temporarily deaf. Karla had hurled a M-180 concussion grenade into the room and the blast put everyone out of commission long enough for her team to steal all the money they wanted without anyone getting in the way.

Karla stood on the loading dock and punched the stopwatch.

"Four minutes!" she hollered.

The other two raiders ran like hell for the counting room, grabbing two bags of money apiece and hauling them back to the hole in the wall.

Engine and siren of their green Plymouth Fury screaming, Axel, Taggart, and Billie were racing up

Wilshire, ignoring a red light and hurtling through the busy intersection at Doheny. Axel was being slammed about in the backseat as if he were riding in a blender. Billie never took his eyes off the road, his heart pounding in his chest as he steered the car. He had to admit he always had a lot more fun when Axel was around.

Taggart had the microphone of the radio transmitter in his big fist. "Unit 21 handle," he bellowed. "Unit 22 assist. Possible 211. Silent. At Cal Deposit, 341 Gregory!" He tossed the mike aside and killed their own siren. In a matter of minutes—the way Rosewood was driving—they would be close to Cal Deposit.

But it wasn't to be. Billie blitzed the corner onto Gregory, taking the turn on two wheels. He almost had to stand up to put enough pressure on the brakes to stop the car before it rammed the one ahead of them.

"Dammit!" he yelled. "A goddamn traffic jam!"

He craned his neck out of the window and peered down the road. "Construction," he said, and belted the wheel in frustration.

"How far to the bank?" demanded Axel.

"Twenty or thirty blocks," said Taggart hopelessly.

All three of them threw open the doors of the car and jumped into the street. The three cops began pounding up the congested street. Quickly, Axel and Billie outdistanced Taggart.

"He's got a weak heart," shouted Billie.

"Yeah," said Axel, "I think he's mentioned that."

They were getting winded, but still they ran on.

135

BEVERLY HILLS COP II

Axel glanced at Rosewood and noticed an enormous bulge under Billie's suitcoat, more or less where his gun should be.

"Billie," gasped Axel, "what you got under there? A lunch pail?"

Rosewood beamed and pulled open his coat. Strapped to his side was an enormous .44 magnum with a barrel as long, it seemed, as an elephant's trunk. "After that shoot-out at the Greek's I figured I could use a little more firepower."

"Jesus, Billie. Who do you think you are? Dirty Harry? We gotta talk, you and me, I mean we *seriously* gotta talk."

They ran another block at full speed, then Axel glanced at his watch and slowed down. "We'll never make it," he said, out of breath, "we need to find some goddamn wheels."

Rosewood was puffing too. He wiped the sweat from his forehead. "You go that way," he said, pointing to a side street. "I'll take the next one up. Meet you in the middle of the next block."

Mendoza wasn't sure why he was getting to his feet. He was dazed; he was deaf. He felt terrible. Maybe he just wanted to get out of there. When Karla kicked him savagely in the head, he decided that he would just stay put.

"Three minutes!" yelled Karla. As she shouted, she pulled the latest cryptogram—this one marked *C* and *D*—from her jumpsuit pocket and placed it on a desk to her side.

On the other side of the hole in the wall, the action was frantic but organized. As soon as a bag was tossed through, the driver of the brown van grabbed it and tossed it into the rear of his truck. A small mountain of money had grown there in under two minutes.

Axel looked like the most inept car thief in the world. He simply ran down the block of the street parallel to Gregory Way furiously rattling the door handles of every car he found. They were all locked. Normally, a locked car door would not have presented much of an obstacle to Axel, but he didn't have time to pop the lock and hot-wire a car.

"Damn!" he shouted in frustration.

Suddenly, behind him, there was the blast of a gargantuan air horn. Axel whipped around and saw Rosewood perched high up in the cab of a cement-mixer truck. The dome was still turning, liquid cement dribbling out into the street. Axel climbed up in the cab. The interior smelled strongly of old, cheap cigars. Pictures of nude women, cut from girlie magazines, were taped to the cracked plastic visor. If one judged from the woman's positions, one would infer that the driver had an amateur's interest in gynecology.

"For Chrissakes, Billie," yelled Axel, "a cement truck?"

"It's all I could find. Don't worry. Nobody saw me take it," he said sincerely.

Billie wrestled the truck into gear and stomped on the gas. With a lurch the behemoth took off down the street, its twin air horns bellowing as if it were an ocean liner setting out to sea.

* * *

At the two-minute warning, the driver of the brown van stopped assisting with the money that was coming through the hole in the wall of Cal Deposit. He swung up behind the wheel of the van and started the engine. Just at that moment, he saw a cement truck come barreling across the wide-open space that surrounded the bank. It was aimed right at him. The driver gaped for a second. It certainly didn't look like a police car—but it did look like trouble. He leaned on the horn of the van.

Inside the building, Karla heard the horn. She didn't hesitate. "Abort!" she yelled.

The two looters dropped their loads of money and dove through the hole in the wall. Karla was right behind them. They jumped as one into the van.

"Son-of-a-bitch!" she yelled as she slammed the door. What the hell could have gone wrong? She glanced out the window and saw the cement truck. "Go!" she ordered.

The tires of the van screamed and it took off across the lot. Rosewood downshifted and swung the wheel, turning his big machine in a wide arc after the van. Axel couldn't do anything but hang on.

The brown van didn't head for the exit to the lot. The driver just gunned his engine and headed straight for the curb. As he bounced over it across the sidewalk and lurched into the road, everyone and everything in the van bounced. Karla banged her head on the roof and fell back on a money bag, splitting it open. Suddenly, the interior of the van was a swirling blizzard of big bucks.

Rosewood's eyes never left the rear of the van. He

floored the cement truck: he was going to go out the way they had, over the curb.

"The curb, Billie. The goddamn curb!" yelled Axel.

"I see it," Billie said in a "no big deal" tone of voice. The cement truck hit the six-inch curb doing sixty. The engine howled as they hit—for a second the big truck was airborne, sailing over the sidewalk and slamming into the street, dragging the underside of the truck on the asphalt. Sparks flew. Rosewood gave it all the gas it could take. The mixer fishtailed wildly and rocketed down the street. Billie had done a magnificent job, except for one small detail. He was on the wrong side of the street—and heading into traffic.

At first, the driver of the shiny new Cadillac couldn't be sure, but it seemed that a giant cement mixer was going about a hundred miles an hour the wrong way down El Camino. It was getting bigger with every second. It did not look as if it was going to stop. The driver of the Caddy didn't think about it anymore, he just reacted, wrenching the wheel of his car wildly to avoid the thundering beast. He did so—but he slammed into the side of a Maserati Biturbo. Parked next to it was a 1976 Datsun. Why, he wondered, did he have to hit the Maserati? He swiveled around in his seat, but the cement mixer was long gone and the driver of the Caddy was beginning to wonder if it had ever actually existed.

Much as Rosewood tried, he couldn't catch the van. He had kept his foot flat on the accelerator, getting every ounce of power he could out of the shrieking engine. But the van was pulling away by the second. Axel shouted over the blaring horn.

"We're losing them, Billie. We'll never catch them in this thing."

Axel shot a glance at the van far ahead up the street. But in his line of sight was also a nice, red Mercedes 450 parked at the corner a little farther up. Now *that* would catch the van.

"Stop, Billie!"

"What?"

"Stop the goddamn truck!"

Rosewood wrestled the lumbering beast to a screaming, rubber-burning stop.

Axel spoke fast. "Get rid of the truck. Hide it somewhere nobody can find it. And don't let anyone see you do it or you won't be a cop tomorrow. I'm going up Coldwater after them."

He jumped from the truck and dashed to the Mercedes. There were two men in the car, dressed and made up in a way that would have, well, excited a certain amount of attention in Detroit. In Beverly Hills they would not have merited a second glance. The older of the two men, Cecil, was wearing a tanktop and shorts—nothing odd about that. But the diamond earring and orange hair was a little out of the ordinary. Likewise, his companion, Edward. His pink lipstick and red-and-green hair was something of an attention-getter.

Axel pulled open the door of the Mercedes, scooped up Cecil, and deposited him on Edward's lap.

"Hi, men," he said, sliding behind the wheel,

firing up the powerful, smooth engine and peeling out, tearing up Coldwater fast. Moving from the cement mixer to the Mercedes was like changing from a bed of nails to a flying carpet.

"This was in our horoscope, Edward," said Cecil calmly.

Edward was less sanguine. "Tell me this isn't happening. Tell me this is not happening," he yelled, somehow in a monotone.

"It's not happening, Edward," said Axel obligingly. "It's a hallucination. All that hair dye has got into your brain."

"Excuse me, sir," said Cecil. "Are you stealing the car or are we being kidnapped?"

Axel didn't answer—he was watching as the van swung left. Axel whipped around the corner. He caught a glimpse of the van disappearing to the right. And Axel went right, flooring the Mercedes.

"You know," said Cecil, "this is sort of exciting."

"He could have taken a cab," said Edward.

Axel had a sinking feeling that he had lost the van—he couldn't catch sight of it anymore. He drove at high speed around the warren of streets in north Beverly Hills, hoping for a glimpse of his prey. But the van was gone.

"Shit," said Axel.

"Go up Tower," said Cecil helpfully. "It's a really lovely street. Garbo used to live on Tower."

"Which one is Tower?"

Cecil pointed to a side street. Axel zoomed off. Halfway up Tower Road, Axel brought the car to a screaming halt. He thought he'd glimpsed something out of the corner of his eye. Then he backed up a hundred yards and saw the brown van parked a few hundred yards down a narrow tree-lined road.

Axel got out of the car and walked a few yards down the street. It was definitely the van. He sprinted back to the Mercedes. "Cecil," said Axel, "I love you, man, I really do."

Cecil looked pleased. "Listen, would you like to come to a party at our house tonight?"

"Nothing big," said Edward, "just a small group. Come any way you want."

Axel smiled. "Some other time. You guys have fun. I gotta go to work now." He pulled the Browning out of his belt, checked the magazine, and slipped a round into the chamber.

Cecil, behind the wheel now, saw the gun and hit the gas, did a Rosewood-style U-turn, and beat it back down Tower Road, not even pausing to look at the house that Greta Garbo used to live in.

CHAPTER
TEN

Axel moved stealthily down the narrow lane, his Browning at his side but ready. He couldn't see anyone in the van, couldn't hear anyone either, but he wanted to be prepared for anything. As he neared the van, he two-handed his gun, holding it out in front of him, ready to shoot. One of the side doors of the van stood ajar. He nudged it open, adrenaline surging through him as he did so.

But the van was empty. Axel felt himself calming down. He holstered his gun and wondered if it was worth having the van dusted for prints. He thought it would probably be a waste of time. Anyone capable of pulling off a robbery at Cal Deposit wasn't going to be stupid enough to leave a fresh set of lifts in the getaway car.

And it was definitely the vehicle they had used. Lying on the grass at his feet was a fifty-dollar bill. People didn't lose money like that unless they were in a hurry and had plenty more. He pocketed the fifty. He'd use it to buy Rosewood and Taggart a drink or something when they nailed the Alphabet bandit.

He looked over the scene. Obviously, they had to drive away from here. There were fresh tire tracks showing a sweeping U-turn just beyond the van. The tracks then went back down the road toward Tower.

Axel followed them back to the main road and saw that they turned to the right, heading farther up into the hills. He followed them for a hundred yards or so, until the mud from the dirt road had worn off the tires. Axel stopped in the middle of the road and looked around him. On either side of the street were tall gates guarding the entrances to grand mansions. Far off, up the long driveway, he could hear music, laughter, and the clink of glasses. Someone was having a party and he hadn't been invited. He wondered if his prey was in there. He glanced at the few cars parked at the gate, and a clue smacked him square in the face. He grinned broadly. A Mercedes was parked on the street and there was no mistaking the ownership: the license plate read "M-Dent." Not *too* obvious, he told himself.

A car came rocketing up Tower and screeched to a halt next to him. Axel dove for cover, his Browning half out of his holster, before he realized Rosewood and Taggart had caught up with him.

"Billie! Taggart! How the hell did you find me?"

"Well," said Billie sheepishly, "we *are* on traffic duty."

"Yeah," said Axel, mystified.

"We got a call to pull over a Mercedes doing ninety on Coldwater. The report said it was being driven by a guy with green hair."

"Ed and Cecil!" said Axel.

"Yeah," growled Taggart. "They said they had just escaped from a black kidnapper-murderer-rapist-car thief. So we knew it had to be you."

Axel laughed and looked back at the mansion. "They're in there," he said.

"*There?*" asked Billie.

Axel nodded at Dent's car. "Got to be."

"And we're going in?"

"Yes," said Axel.

"We can't go in there," said Taggart, aghast. "It's the Playboy Mansion."

"I thought you were a playboy, Taggart?" Axel swung open the gate and walked up the drive toward the party that was being held on the terrace.

Behind him, Axel heard Taggart groan. "I don't know if my heart can stand this."

They were stopped in the foyer of the mansion by a pert young woman who sat behind a table, a guest list in front of her. A sign on the table said: "Playboy Welcomes Heart Fund for Millions." Axel walked right by her as if she didn't exist. She put out a hand and caught him by the sleeve. Rosewood and Taggart stopped and stared, awestruck at the mansion. And this was just the entrance hall.

"Don't touch me, Debra," he said, reading her name off a tag she had pinned to the lapel of her jacket, "you don't know where I've been."

Debra refused to be charmed. She had encountered gate-crashers before. "Your name, please?"

Axel did a double take. "You're kidding, right?"

Debra wasn't kidding and she was looking around to see if one of the plainclothes security men might be looking her way.

"I was told there would be no mention of names," said Axel in disbelief.

Debra shook her head. "I'm sorry, but I can't admit anyone whose name does not appear on this list."

Axel was getting cranked up. He raised his voice slightly and acted most put out. "I can't have my name appearing on a list like that. No one is supposed to know I'm here. I only agreed to come here on the explicit promise that no one would know. I can't believe this."

He turned to Rosewood and Taggart. "Can you believe this? She wants to put my name on the list." Taggart looked away. Rosewood did his best to play along.

"Heh," he said, and shrugged. More than that he couldn't manage. He would have liked to say, "The nerve of some people," but he wasn't sure he could say it without choking. Rosewood looked beyond the entrance hall. In the large living room a few feet away there were at least two hundred and fifty thousand of the prettiest women he had ever seen in his life.

Axel seemed to fume with frustration. "If my name appears on that list, then everybody would know that I'm here. That is not what I was promised—"

"I'm sorry, sir, but—"

Axel steamrolled over her objections. "And without that promise I would not have come all the way out here from New York. This was supposed to be private and relaxed with nobody hassling me and this is what I get." He looked back at Rosewood, hoping for a little more support this time. But Rosewood didn't care if they got in. He was happy just to stand there staring.

"I'm sorry," Debra started to explain.

Axel threw up his hands. "Don't explain it to me.

147

Explain it to your boss. Explain it to him when he asks you why he's getting beaten to death on the *Today Show*."

Holy shit, thought Debra. It was that black guy from the "Today Show." She *knew* he looked familiar, sort of. "The *Today Show* . . . You're, uh . . . uh. I'm awfully sorry, Mr. . . ."

"Don't mention it," said Axel affably. "And don't write it down on the list." He pointed to Rosewood and Taggart. "And don't put their names down. Or don't you recognize them either?" he kept up in a mocking tone.

Oh God, thought Taggart, *he's going to make me Gerald Ford again.*

Again Debra groped for a name. She had never seen the "Today Show." She knew that there was a funny weatherman. . . . She shook her head. "I'm sorry, I don't."

Axel looked at her curiously. "Debra, what time do you get up in the morning?"

She gulped. This was like meeting a famous author at the mansion and being forced to admit that she hadn't read his latest best-seller. "Actually, I usually work really late," she said apologetically, "and then I exercise to a video. . . ."

Axel knew they were in. He started to walk away. "I'd like to hear a lot more about your private life, Debra, but first I better go say hello to your boss."

Rosewood and Taggart hustled along behind him, as if afraid of losing him in the crowd. They walked through the lavish, paneled living room and out on to the terrace. There was a buffet table at one end and waiters circulated in the crowd with trays of drinks and canapes. People leaned against the railing of the terrace, chatting and laughing, or simply looking out at the beautiful gardens, the fountains and grottoes, and the spectacular view of Los Angeles beyond.

Rosewood, Taggart, and Axel were looking at the women. There seemed to be swarms of beauties everywhere they looked. Axel closed his eyes for a moment, then opened them, looking down and whispering to his crotch.

"This is the moment I always promised you," he said solemnly. "It may not happen again, so I want you to remember everything you see."

Rosewood was wondering why parties at his house never seemed to be like this.

Taggart looked at the women and sighed to himself. If he was going to die, it might as well be here. It would give him the opportunity to get used to what heaven was like.

Axel spoke to them like a coach. "Don't forget, we *are* supposed to be working here."

"What are we supposed to be looking for?" asked Rosewood as his eyes zeroed in on a beautiful blonde.

"Whoever was in the van is in here somewhere."

"But we don't know what they look like."

"Yeah," said Taggart, his eyes locking on Rosewood's blonde. "It could be anyone." He would have dearly liked to interrogate her—preferably in a motel.

"Dent's here. Let's see who we can connect up to

him. Mill around. Ask questions. You guys are supposed to be detectives. Detect!" Axel walked away. He too had spotted a couple of women he would like to have a chat with.

"Right," said Rosewood, his gaze shifting to what he imagined was the most beautiful Asian girl in Los Angeles. He had always been interested in the East. "I think I have a suspect," he said to Taggart.

He walked up to the Asian girl. "Excuse me, miss. I'd like to ask you a few questions. . . ."

The girl's brown, almond-shaped eyes swept over him. "The answers are all no." She walked away, leaving Rosewood, mouth open, trying to think of something to say.

"Look, Billie," said Taggart, trying to be helpful, "you can't come on like Dirty Harry in here. You gotta blend in. Be part of the atmosphere. You know, mellow and laid back." He glanced over at the blonde both of them had spotted earlier. "See her? I'll show you what I mean." Taggart began to stroll toward the young woman and forced himself not to look down the front of her dress.

"See, Billie," he said confidently, "it may have been a few years since I've been on the scene, but I think I can still handle it. It's all in your rap, you know what I mean."

Billie knew what he meant. Taggart meant he was going to make a fool of himself.

"Hi," Taggart said to the girl. He felt he was being very smooth, very suave.

The girl glanced at and then through him.

"I'm Jack and I'm a Taurus. What's your sign?"

"Dollars," she said, walking away.

Axel didn't want to have any fun. He had spotted Dent and Thomopolis at the edge of the terrace. They were engrossed in conversation. It was hard to say which of the two looked less pleased.

"You don't have the money," Thomopolis hissed. "And you need more time. I'll give you more time. One day. How's that?"

"*One* day—"

"That's what I said." Thomopolis's voice and eyes were cold. "You get the money or you lose everything. Is that clear?"

Suddenly, Axel slapped Dent on the back. Dent turned swiftly.

"Max!" said Axel, acting surprised and delighted to see the man. "How'd you get in here? You look great for a cheap thug." Axel took one of Dent's lapels between his thumb and forefinger and rubbed it, appraising the quality of the material like a tailor. "This is a great suit. A really intelligent fabric."

"Now that you've ruined it," said Dent through clenched teeth, "I can arrange to have you buried in it."

Axel ignored him. He turned to Thomopolis. "And you're—I can never pronounce that name."

"Thomopolis," said Thomopolis stiffly.

Axel was talking a little louder than the rest of the crowd, and heads began to turn in their direction. A plainclothesman made his way discreetly over to them.

"Some trouble, gentlemen?"

"No trouble," said Axel. "I was just asking the boys here about the business they were planning? What is it, Max? Guns or drugs?"

"I don't know who this person is," said Dent to the security man, "but he is annoying us."

"I have only just begun to annoy you, Maxie."

"Would you do something about this man, please?" Dent may have said *please,* but there was no question that he was giving the security man an order.

Axel spotted Hugh Hefner standing a few yards away. He still hadn't noticed the set-to that was developing on his terrace.

Axel was shouting now. "You ought to be a little more careful with your guest list." Axel poked Dent in the chest. "This man tries to kill cops."

The guard glanced nervously at Hefner, who was now looking his way. "Now, let's not have any trouble . . ."

"Hey, Hef," Axel continued, calling toward him, "I better give you a little background on your guest. The man shoots cops. You really don't want him hanging around here. It looks bad to the neighbors."

Hefner disengaged himself from the group of friends he had been chatting with. He walked over to Axel and Dent. Security men were beginning to converge on the scene.

Hefner looked coldly at Axel and then at Dent. "I don't know him or you. I just opened the house for a charity. I think you had all better go." Hefner turned to the guards. "See them all out."

Dent looked outraged. "I happen to be a major contributor to this—"

Hefner cut him off. "And we're very grateful. Good-bye." Hefner returned to his guests as the security men started hustling Dent and Axel toward the door. Axel bumped up against Max as they were escorted off the premises. Axel pushed him roughly away. "Get off me, man," he said. Dent stepped away. "I can see myself out," he said to the guards. He walked through the house, Karla appearing at his side.

"Hey, Karla," shouted Axel, "drop by the house for that shave I owe you . . ."

As Dent and Karla were going through the gate, she hissed: "I want him."

"No. He's deliberately provoking me. He wants us to come after him. We'll go ahead as planned. Get Cain. Prepare the next operation."

Taggart and Rosewood morosely followed Axel out of the mansion. Rosewood paused to look back at the splendid building. Well, he had had a little glimpse of paradise. . . .

CHAPTER
ELEVEN

Axel seemed unconcerned about being bounced out of the Playboy Mansion. He had gotten what he wanted. As the Plymouth pulled away from the gates, Rosewood at the wheel, Axel pulled a slim, finely made wallet from his pocket, flipped it open, and started going through it. No money. *What a cheapskate,* thought Axel—then he remembered hearing somewhere that really rich people never carried any money on them. They always had a flunky around to pay the bills, or they stuck some sucker with the tab.

But then again, Axel wondered, if Dent was so rich, why the hell would he be mixed up in large-scale theft?

Rosewood glanced at Axel and saw Dent's driver's license. His eyes grew wide. "You've got Dent's wallet."

Taggart, in the back, threw himself forward. "You picked Dent's *pocket*?" he said in disbelief.

"Hey, Taggart, I wasn't born a cop."

Taggart nodded wearily and finished the thought for him. "I know, I know. You fractured an occasional law when you were a kid."

Lutz was about to bust a gut. Not only did he have no leads in the Adrianos' robbery, one of his police

156

captains fighting for his life in an IC unit, a wild robbery of the most secure banking facility west of the Rockies—*now* he had some unknown vigilante out there foiling major crimes with a cement truck.

"A cement truck," he growled, looking around his office. He looked at Rosewood. "A cement truck."

Rosewood shrugged, as if to say, "Don't look at me."

Lutz's beady eyes swiveled over to Taggart. "A cement truck?"

"Never saw it, Chief," mumbled Taggart.

Mayor Egan, once again in the office, spoke up. "I don't think the cement truck is really that important, Harold."

Lutz was about to say that he didn't give a good goddamn what his opinion was, but then he realized that the mayor did the hiring and firing of police chiefs in Beverly Hills and decided that it wouldn't be good politics to mouth off at him.

Instead, Lutz's eyes lighted on Biddle. "A cement truck, Biddle?"

Biddle, supposedly in command of the Alphabet bandit case, knew he had to say something. "Well," he said nervously, "I have a theory on that, Chief. I think the cement truck was a tactical decoy." Biddle hadn't thought of that until a second before, but it sounded good to him.

It didn't sound so good to Lutz. "A decoy?"

"Yes," said Biddle, warming to his theory. "It was a diversion to protect the criminal's getaway."

Lutz sighed. How was it he had picked such a

bonehead for a protégé? "Biddle, whoever was in that cement truck *foiled* the goddamned crime."

Quickly, Biddle abandoned his beloved theory. "Say, now that *is* a point, Chief," he said in frank admiration.

Lutz turned to Axel. "And just what the hell were you doing there?"

Axel was cool. "Just passing by. I'm a cop, aren't I? Did you call Inspector Todd in Detroit?"

"Yeah, I called. Your inspector doesn't seem to like you very much."

"I'm sorry to hear that," said Axel evenly. "If I wanted to be loved, I'd have been a fireman."

"Look, Harold," said Egan, "the fact remains that whatever the explanation, the robbery was halted and most of the money was saved."

"By some unknown lunatic in a cement truck," said Lutz. That cement truck really annoyed him.

"If I were you," Egan continued, "I would concentrate on cracking these codes and finding out where the *E* crime will be."

"How the hell are we supposed to . . ." said Lutz helplessly.

It was just like in the cartoons. It seemed to Axel that a little light bulb lit up just above his head. "Wait," he said.

"What for?" demanded Lutz.

"We've been assuming that these crimes have had letters attached to them just for the hell of it."

"Yes," said Biddle, anxious to reassert his control over the case. "That's why it's called the Alphabet bandit case."

"Yeah, but that's wrong," said Axel.

"No it isn't," said Biddle.

"No. Biddle, check this out. *A* was for Adriano's. *B* was for Bogomil. *C* and *D* were for—"

"Cal Deposit," filled in Egan.

"So the next crime," said Axel, "will be committed at an *E* or possibly an *E-F* location."

"Oh," said Biddle. "That makes sense."

"How many prime targets can there be starting with the letter *E*?" said Egan. "Well, I think you've done some fine work, gentlemen." He pointedly directed his words to Taggart, Rosewood, and Axel, excluding Biddle and Lutz. "Keep it up. I'll see you later, Harold," he said, making for the door.

Axel thought this might be a good time to get lost himself. He followed the mayor down the hall. Rosewood and Taggart smiled nervously. Should they go or should they stay? Surely Lutz would have to put them back on the case.

"Okay," said Lutz. He was very angry that he had to accept Axel's theory, but it did seem plausible. He started rapping out orders. "Check every possible *E* crime location in Beverly Hills. Maps, phone books. Try the . . . uh . . ."

"Library," supplied Rosewood obligingly.

"Library," said Lutz. "Biddle, go push the FBI on cracking that code."

Biddle fled.

Lutz flopped down in his desk chair and sighed. He picked up the report on the Cal Deposit robbery and wondered who the hell had driven that cement truck. A minute of deep thought passed before he realized that Taggart and Rosewood were still in his office. They were sitting very quietly, like kids called in before the principal.

"What the hell are you waiting for?" he snarled.

"Well," said Taggart, swallowing, "we were wondering if we—"

Lutz cut him off. Here was a chance to vent some of the anger that had grown to dangerously high levels in his system. "You two are just traffic cops. Get out of here. And stay the hell away from Foley or I'll jail both of you."

If it had been up to Taggart, he would have stayed away from Axel. It's just that Axel wouldn't stay away from him and Billie. He was sitting in the backseat of their car, waiting for them.

"Weren't you supposed to leave for Detroit today?" asked Taggart brusquely, sliding in behind the wheel of the car.

"Yeah," said Axel. "At noon. But we have to go to Century City to see Mr. Bernstein the accountant."

"You're never going to make it," said Rosewood. He was trying to get comfortable in the front seat, but the cannon he was wearing under his coat made it hard to sit straight. "You are going to be fired."

Axel shrugged. "Hell, we started this together and we'll finish it together. Find out if Sidney Bernstein owns a car."

Rosewood tapped the information into the little computer mounted on the dash of the car. The screen lit up. "Yeah," he said. "Eighty-six Mercedes. License number CRL-507."

"You're on traffic, right?"

"Right," said Taggart. Man, how he hated that Lutz.

"Then let's give out some tickets. Pass me your ticket book."

"Axel, please . . ."

Axel vaulted forward and pulled the ticket book out of the glove compartment. He clicked the point of a ballpoint pen and began scribbling in the ticket book. By the time they had made the ten-minute drive to the Century City offices of Sidney Bernstein, accountant to the stars, Mr. Bernstein had racked up twenty-five parking violations dating back a year.

Century City looked like something from a sci-fi movie. Tall, mirrored monolithic buildings were clustered together, towering over the rest of the city. There was a complex of ramps and escalators at ground level that moved people in and out of the office towers. The offices themselves, all of them luxurious, housed the money men and movers and shakers that made things happen not just in Los Angeles but around the world. Stepping into the elegant foyer of Bernstein's office, Axel knew instantly that this was where the big boys played. Pull a string here and someone in Hong Kong or Paris or Zurich jumped.

But that didn't bother Axel. He was coming to bust Bernstein for traffic violations.

He waved his badge at the secretary, a young woman who looked as if she had just stepped out of the pages of *Vogue*. "Foley, B.H.P.D.," he said, all business. "Bernstein in?"

"Ah . . ." said the secretary.

"Never mind," Axel said, walking by her. "We'll find him."

Bernstein sat behind a huge polished desk, a giant picture window behind him giving an overwhelming view of Los Angeles. He looked as surprised as his secretary when Axel burst into the room flashing his badge.

"How did you get in here?" he asked, more surprised than angry.

"Beverly Hills Police Department, special warrant detail. Are you Sidney Bernstein, owner of an eighty-six Mercedes CRL-507?"

"Has it been stolen?"

"Nope."

"Thank God," said Bernstein, falling back in his deeply cushioned desk chair.

"I wouldn't thank the man so fast," said Axel, "I've got a warrant for your arrest. . . ."

Taggart, standing behind Axel, felt a sharp pain in his chest.

"What!" shouted Bernstein. It was that goddamn tax shelter he had set up in the Cayman Islands, he thought. He told himself he *knew* he never should have done that. . . .

"Yeah, like you didn't know you got twenty-five parking tickets, Bernstein. Some are a year old."

Bernstein felt a warm feeling course through him. *Parking tickets!* Now he knew what it was like to get a last-minute reprieve before execution.

"But . . ." he said.

"Yeah, I know," said Axel, "you never got any

parking tickets. That's what we always hear, right, guys?"

"Right," parroted Rosewood loyally.

Bernstein was mystified. He had really never received a parking ticket. "It's absurd," he said.

Axel thrust a fistful of tickets at him. "What are these, Bernstein? Green stamps?"

"But there's been a mistake. If I'd received a parking ticket, I'd have paid it."

"Happens sometimes, Sid," said Axel. "Wind blows 'em off the car, you forget about them. Whatever. We gotta take you in."

Bernstein paled. "You're kidding."

"'Fraid not." He turned to Rosewood. "Gimme your cuffs."

"Ah . . . ah . . ." stammered Bernstein, "isn't there some way we can avoid this unpleasantness, gentlemen?"

Axel smiled and sat on the edge of the desk. "Sometimes we can make a special arrangement."

Bernstein nodded. "I thought so," he said. "How much?"

Axel looked up at the ceiling. "Let's see . . . twenty-five tickets . . . Two hundred should cover it."

Cheap cop, thought Bernstein. He spent two hundred bucks on lunch. He flipped open his wallet and handed over two crisp hundred-dollar bills.

"Very nice doing business with you, Officer," said Bernstein. "Now if you'll let me get back to—"

"One thing, Sid," interrupted Axel. "We gotta wipe out the records in the computer. If we don't, this little transaction might come back to haunt us all. Can I use your phone?"

"You can use the one at the secretary's desk," said Bernstein.

"Use your head, Sid. Do you want her to know what just came down in here? I gotta take out an arrest record and fix the tickets."

"Okay," said Bernstein. "Use the phone in here."

Axel picked up the phone and dialed two numbers, then stopped. "Mr. Bernstein, I'm sure that a man of your sophistication understands that my contact in the computer room wouldn't want his name mentioned in front of strangers. Like you."

"I understand completely," said Bernstein. Anything to get these guys out of here.

"Then would you mind waiting outside with my partners? Just a second while I talk to him?"

What the hell is he up to? wondered Taggart, his arm throbbing painfully.

"Of course," said Bernstein.

Billie held the door open for him like the doorman at a swank hotel.

Nice man, that Bernstein, thought Axel. He picked up the phone and dialed a number. While it rang, he pulled the phone to the farthest point of the extension cord and opened some drawers in the filing cabinet that stood against one wall of the room. He found Dent's file with relative ease. He flipped it open and saw that Bernstein had been doing a lot of work for Dent recently.

It seemed that Dent was moving and had put the details in his accountant's hands—but he wasn't moving from Bel Air to Holmby Hills. Maxwell Dent appeared to be leaving Beverly Hills for Costa Rica. There were shipping bills and receipts for furniture, cars, and appliances all transported to San José, Costa Rica. Axel had never been to Costa Rica and he had no way of knowing if San José was a nice place, but Axel doubted that it was any nicer than Beverly Hills. And Dent was definitely going for a while: there was an application for permanent resident status. Dent wasn't coming back. The last piece of paper in Dent's file was a manifest listing the contents of a shipment of heavy oil equipment— chains, pipes, casings—that was being *airfreighted* to San José. Why the hell would anyone airfreight stuff like that? Axel felt a little jolt. The stuff was leaving LAX that day.

He slid the file back in place, closed the drawer, and waited for his call to be answered. Jan Bogomil picked up. Axel spoke fast.

"It's me," he said. "What you got?"

"It's strange, Axel," she said. "Before 1978 everything's blank, classified. But his policy date was 1974, so I checked our office in London and found out that Dent was the cultural attaché at the East German embassy in Honduras."

"Honduras? Cultural attaché? I bet they can't get enough of that East German culture down there in Honduras. What does all this look like to you?"

"Spies," said Jan. "But he isn't a spy anymore. He's built quite an empire. The shooting club, a racetrack, a drilling rig company, an oil company."

"Oil company?"

"That's his biggest business. But listen, Axel, these records seem to show that Dent's in financial trouble."

That was what Axel wanted to hear. In his mind the pieces of the puzzle were beginning to fit together. "Tell me about it."

"He's let his insurance lapse on everything in the last six months, on Dent Petroleum, on the shooting club—on everything except for one thing."

"What is it?"

"The racetrack. Empyrean Fields. He's got a huge policy on that one, all paid up."

"Empyrean with an *E*," said Axel. "Hey, Jan . . ."

"What?"

Axel smiled. "When your father wakes up, tell him you found his man."

Axel zoomed through the reception area on his way to the door. "Everything's in order, Sidney. I'll just tear these up," he said, waving the tickets at him. "Sorry about the misunderstanding."

"My pleasure, Officer . . ."

Axel filled Taggart and Rosewood in on the details as they drove at top speed through the streets. Axel also had the latest code on his lap and he was working on it as if trying to untie a particularly tight knot. But he was getting somewhere. This code was a lot easier than the others. In fact Axel had seen ones like it before.

"But he wouldn't rob his own racetrack," said Rosewood, mystified.

"If it's insured he might."

"Steal his own money and then collect the insurance on it," said Taggart in disgust. "Some people are really greedy."

"He's going for more than that, Taggart," said Axel. He didn't look up from the code.

"What? The oil business he seems to be starting in Costa Rica?"

"My hunch is that we won't find any oil-field equipment if we find Dent."

"*If* we find Dent?" said Rosewood.

"I have a feeling the man is leaving tonight. Once he gets to Central America, he's gone." Suddenly Axel grinned broadly. "Hey," he said. "Look!"

He held up the code.

"Son-of-a-bitch," said Taggart excitedly, "you broke it. You beat the computer."

"What's it say?" demanded Rosewood.

Axel laughed. "*Chingen su madre, perros.* Screw you, cops! Signed Carlos."

"Carlos?"

"Carlos?" echoed Taggart. "Charles . . . Cain. The bandit is Cain. How the hell did you break that code, Axel?"

"Cain changed his name, right? Probably a poor kid who didn't want to grow up to be a poor man. Where you got poor people, you are sure to find the numbers racket." He showed the code to Taggart. "This is an old numbers code. They never wrote anything down straight. So they gave numbers to alphabet letters. *01* is *A* and right down the line to *Z*. Simple. Any cop over the age of fifty in Detroit, New York, Chicago would have recognized it."

"See, that's the problem," said Taggart, "not enough poor people in Beverly Hills."

"So it's definitely Cain," said Rosewood.

"I doubt it," said Axel. "The other codes have been much harder. This is a different code, much easier. Whoever wrote this . . . it looks like they wanted us to break it. It's too simple."

"How the hell did you know that old numbers code?" asked Rosewood. "You're not an old cop. Did you run numbers when you were a kid?"

Axel laughed. Taggart spoke for him. "Hell, Billie, he wasn't born a cop, you know . . ."

"Yeah, yeah, I know, he fractured an occasional law."

"Very good, boys," said Axel, grinning from ear to ear. "Now, Billie, drive this thing!"

CHAPTER TWELVE

Charles "Chip" Cain was sitting in the fold-up seat in the passenger compartment of Max Dent's Mercedes limousine. He was very nervous, but not because Dent was giving him hell for all the things that had gone wrong recently. Quite the opposite. Dent was being extremely reasonable and understanding. That chilled Cain to the bone.

"I just don't know what happened on the Cal Deposit hit, Max. There's no way anyone tipped the cops off."

The door of the luxurious vehicle opened and Karla took her place next to Dent. She was wearing a white leather jumpsuit. In contrast to Cain, she did not look nervous. In fact, she looked as if she didn't have a care in the world.

"Yes," said Dent evenly, "it is a mystery to me too. How about the Foley hit? That wasn't handled very well, was it?"

"No," said Cain. "It wasn't." *Why didn't the son-of-a-bitch get mad?* All this understanding was frightening him to death.

Dent noticed that Cain was almost trembling in the little seat. "Calm down, Charles. It's all right. Everybody makes mistakes from time to time."

"I'm sorry, Max."

"This time, Charles," Dent said, "I would like you to go along personally and make absolutely certain nothing goes wrong."

Cain hesitated a moment.

"Have you a problem with that, Charles?"

"No, of course not. I'm on the team . . ."

"That's good, Charles," said Dent smoothly. "I'm sure that everything will go off just as planned." He glanced at Karla and then handed her the latest note. The large block letter *E* was stamped on the outside of the envelope.

"Get in the van," said Dent calmly. "Give me a minute, then hit it hard."

Karla opened the door of the van. "Come on," she said to Cain.

"Good-bye, Charles," said Dent. "And good luck."

"Nothing will go wrong, Max. I give you my word."

"Good," said Dent, closing the door.

The eighth race was just about to begin when Dent took his place in his private box at the Empyrean Fields racetrack. Nikos Thomopolis was waiting for him, two of his goons standing at the door of the box watching every move around them, like the secret service protecting a foreign dignitary.

"I apologize for being late, Nikos. I was attending to some last-minute details."

Thomopolis got straight to the point. "I hope one of the details was money."

Dent nodded. "It was."

"Have you got it?" asked the Greek bluntly.

Technically Dent didn't, but he wasn't going to bore Thomopolis with the details. He would have the money in a matter of minutes.

"Have you got it?" asked Thomopolis testily.

"Of course I have."

"Good." Thomopolis started to rise.

"Ah, Nikos . . ." Dent motioned for him to sit down again.

"What?"

"I assume that you have the merchandise."

Thomopolis almost laughed. "I always have the merchandise."

"Good, Nikos." Dent shook Thomopolis's hand. "I will be seeing you shortly."

"With the money," said Nikos.

Dent nodded. "With the money."

Thomopolis stood up and instantly his gunmen were by his side. Without another word, the arms merchant left the box.

By the time the eighth race had been run, the money of unlucky bettors was pouring into the counting room, which was in on a floor closed to the public. There were a half-dozen men and women in the room, all of them sitting at desks, and each desk was filled with towering stacks of bills. Grubby ones from the two-dollar windows running all the way up to razor-sharp five-hundred and thousand-dollar bills from the high rollers.

There were twelve closed-circuit television cameras mounted on brackets high up on the walls. These scanned the counting room constantly, relaying their pictures to the security room a few doors away. Two uniformed security officers sat behind the bank of monitors idly watching Dent's money being counted. Everything was going along normally, just the way it always did.

A janitor in overalls was working deep within the building. He pushed a trash collector down a narrow hall, the can overflowing with racing forms, torn-up tickets, beer cups. He stopped at a service elevator, pressed the call button, and when the doors opened, he stepped inside. He hauled his trash collector in behind him. The doors closed.

When the elevator was between floors, the janitor hit the emergency stop button, bringing the car to a lurching halt. Quickly he taped the button down, holding the elevator in place. He clambered up on his trash can, pushed open the hatch in the roof of the cab, and hauled himself onto the roof of the elevator.

The elevator had come to a stop next to a circuit box. He opened it and found a thick red cable, pulled a sharp knife out of his pocket, and started slicing the insulation off the cable. He quickly laid bare the copper wires in the center. From a pocket of his overalls he took a tiny, six-inch-square Sony video recorder. It contained precisely four minutes of prerecorded tape. He wired the unit to the cable, checked his watch, and then started the unit.

In the security room, one guard noticed a slight blip on the TV screens watching the counting room. He thought nothing of it. It lasted less than a second and there, on the screen, were the counters working away. What he didn't know was that he was watching a tape that the "janitor" had wired into the system. In the counting room itself, all hell was about to break loose.

The ninth and final race was about to begin when three uniformed security guards appeared in the betting area walking toward the counting room. No one noticed them, and if they did, no one noticed that all three were wearing heavy dark glasses and that the tallest of the three was a woman.

Karla had tucked her long blond hair under the cap, she had removed her makeup, and the glasses more or less obscured her face. Her companions were Cain and Jack May. Sadly, Willie couldn't be with them. Dent felt that he had screwed up the hit on Axel too badly to be part of the team anymore. His body would wash up near Manhattan Beach a few days later.

Karla rapped on the door of the counting room. A small hatch in the door opened and Jack Stiles, the counting-room chief, glanced out. He unlocked the door and the three security guards stepped in. He checked their plastic ID cards against a list of names on a clipboard. Karla's eyes flashed to the .38 holstered on his hip.

"Okay," said Stiles, "you're in. This way." He led them down a narrow hall to a heavy steel door with the words *Counting Room* stenciled on it in black letters. He unlocked the door and they walked in. None of the counters gave them a second glance.

Karla reached into the money sack she had been

carrying and slipped on a pair of gloves. Then she tossed out three small breathing masks with a canister attached to the side of each. Each canister held five minutes of oxygen.

Stiles happened to look their way. "What the hell are you doing?" he asked as Karla slipped on her mask. Her answer to his question was the blow of a blackjack just behind his ear. He went down fast. Calmly, Karla pulled another device out of her bag of tricks. It looked like a small fire extinguisher. She ripped a cord on its side and suddenly the counting room was filled with a noxious fog. Counters stood up and coughed and gagged. A couple stumbled toward the door. They never made it. In seconds, the knockout gas had done its job. Every counter was out cold.

Quickly, May and Cain started moving around the room and stuffing armfuls of cash into Karla's moneybag. In three minutes they had stripped the room bare. The bag was full. Karla knelt next to Stiles, took out his .38, and, rising, faced Cain.

"What the hell are you up to?" demanded Cain, his voice muffled and distorted behind the mask. "We don't have much time—"

"Good-bye, Charles," said Karla. The gun boomed in her hand as the bullet hit Charles Cain dead center in the heart. He was dead before he hit the ground.

May watched the murder of Cain in complete disbelief. For a second he couldn't move. He could hardly think. But he did manage to form one very important thought: *I'm next*. He jumped at Karla, trying to get the gun out of her hand. But he never made it. The .38 roared again and Karla's unerring aim sent a bullet slamming into May's astonished face. She hit him right between the eyes.

She checked her watch, placed the gun in Stiles's hand, and fired one last round. The slug buried itself in the wall. Then she moved to Cain. She removed the final alphabet letter from her breast pocket and shoved it into Cain's uniform. *Behold the Alphabet bandit,* she thought.

Then she started undressing. She stripped off the security-guard uniform, revealing a black silk cocktail dress. She pulled off her hat, and blond hair cascaded to her shoulders. She stuffed her discarded uniform in the moneybag and dragged the heavy load to the door of the counting room.

She stepped into the hallway just as the janitor passed. "Trash, ma'am?" he said with a grin.

"Yes." She smiled, showing perfect white teeth. "But for God's sake, don't incinerate it."

The janitor tossed the bag in the collector and went on his way. A minute later, Karla slipped into Dent's VIP box.

She sipped a drink. She was fairly panting with excitement. The robbery, the killings, the whole campaign finally complete. She mopped the sweat from her brow. She was excited, adrenaline pumping.

Dent looked away from the track. "Did our horse come in?"

"Yes," said Karla, with a little smile. "Cain's did not, I'm afraid."

As Dent escorted Karla toward the exit, the film in the Sony ran out. The guards stared dumbfounded at the monitor. It looked as if there had been a massacre in the counting room. "Jesus," one breathed. Another pressed an alarm.

CHAPTER
THIRTEEN

In the unmarked green Plymouth B.H.P.D. unit, Axel, Rosewood, and Taggart came careening into the vast parking lot that fronted the pavilion of the Empyrean Fields racetrack. The ninth race had been run and bettors—happy if the ponies had run their way, or down if they had just dropped a month's rent—were swarming through the lot trying to get to their cars. Some were anxious to go out on the town and celebrate with their winnings. Others walked glumly, wondering how they were going to explain this to their wives or husbands.

Rosewood hardly slowed down. The crowd threw itself out of the way as the car zoomed through the lot. Just to let them know this was official, not just a bunch of high-spirited high rollers, Taggart hit the siren.

It was then that Axel noticed that there were other sirens going. Ahead of him, by the main entrance of the clubhouse, were a dozen black-and-whites, their lights flashing. Behind them, at the main gates, a half-dozen more were charging into the parking lot, following the same twisting route that Axel had.

They dumped the car and dashed into the building. It was easy to see where the action was. All you had to do was follow the crowd of cops. Axel, with

Taggart and Rosewood close behind, managed to elbow his way into the counting room.

The gassed employees had been taken away to first-aid stations within the racetrack itself—all of them except Jack Stiles, the counting-room chief, who stood by Lutz's side. The young man was a little unsteady on his feet and smiled self-consciously, as if not quite sure what the hell everybody was talking about.

Lying at Lutz's feet, like trophies from a big-game hunt, were two bodies, covered by sheets.

Axel burst in just as an impromptu news conference was getting under way. For a second, Axel imagined that the entire press corps of Los Angeles had been tipped off to the crime, but then he realized that a number of local TV stations would have been broadcasting the day's races and virtually every paper would have had a reporter at Empyrean Fields. A lot of crime reporters ended their working lives covering the track, so Lutz—to his obvious delight—had a perfect audience. And the cherry on the cake was that Mayor Egan just happened to have been at the track that afternoon with some visiting big shots. Lutz couldn't have planned his dramatic announcement better.

It was perfect. The press conference would take place at the crime scene, the bodies of the two perpetrators still in plain view. The young hero who had foiled the crime was at hand—Lutz was going to make the evening news from coast to coast. The job of chief of the B.H.P.D. was his for as long as he wanted it. Now, he could *really* run things his way.

The reporters were hollering questions, but Lutz

took his time, savoring the attention. When he judged the moment to be right, he held up his hand for silence.

"Calm down," he hollered. "Calm down."

"Chief Lutz!" shouted a reporter.

Lutz shook his head. "No questions. I'm just going to make a brief statement. We are confident that we have identified the so-called Alphabet bandit. He is Charles Cain, a convicted criminal." Lutz raised his voice. "There will be no *F* crime." There was a little applause at that announcement.

Please, Biddle pleaded with God, *please let him mention my name*. It had been his case, after all. He hadn't done a damn thing to crack it, but still . . .

Lutz beamed at the applause. "Cain was shot at the scene of this robbery by"—he turned to Stiles, who blushed—"Security Chief Jack Stiles." Stiles shook his head. Anyone who noticed that thought he was probably being modest. But the truth of it was, he didn't remember shooting anyone. He also remembered three guards coming through the door. Where was the third guy? The guy with the sack. He was still in a fog, but it didn't make any sense. Stiles managed to slip out of the glare of the TV lights, leaving the limelight to Lutz.

"Our own team cracked Cain's code this afternoon. The notes were signed Carlos. Which, as you all know, is Charles in Spanish—"

Taggart and Rosewood shot disgusted looks at Axel.

"C'mon," said Axel, "let's get the hell out of here."

Outside the counting room, a couple of Empyrean

Fields security guards were congratulating Jack Stiles. Stiles seemed uncomfortable with the adulation.

"Way to go, Jack," said one of them, patting him on the back.

"Yeah, that's okay, fellas," said Stiles nervously.

Axel stopped.

"C'mon, Jack," said another burly guard. "I'da been scared to death. You, you're a hero, ferchrissakes."

"Yeah . . . I just got one question," said Stiles. "What happened to the money?"

Axel was all ears.

"Money?" said one of the guards. "What do you mean, what happened to the money?"

Axel motioned Taggart and Rosewood to follow him. "Something very strange is going on here," he said. "That Stiles is no fool. He didn't shoot anybody . . . and he knows the money is gone. If Cain's the Alphabet bandit, who took the money? His ghost?"

"And where's Dent?" asked Taggart through a cloud of cigar smoke.

They had left the main building and were walking in the paddock area. Grooms and hotwalkers were taking the racehorses back to their stables at the close of the day's racing. Rosewood stopped in front of a closed stable door.

"Wait," he said, "what are you guys saying?"

Axel kept walking. "It was a setup," said Axel.

"Billie," said Taggart, "you are getting mud all over your shoes."

A wide stream of reddish water was coursing out

from under the door of the stall, swirling gracefully around Rosewood's shoes and ankles and into a drain nearby. "Heck," said Rosewood, and picked up his pace trying to catch up with Axel and Taggart.

"You said he was shipping out to South America?" asked Taggart, trying to work out the problem the way Axel had worked out the code.

"No law against that? And where is he keeping the stuff, anyway?"

"We could pull Dent in . . ."

"On what grounds? Besides, put out an APB on a black Mercedes limo in this town . . ." Axel didn't have to finish his thought. There were more Mercedes in Beverly Hills than in the factory in Stuttgart.

Axel stopped and stared at Billie's soaked shoes and socks. "Where did that come from?"

Rosewood gestured. "Back there."

Axel had seen red mud like that before. On Andrew Bogomil's running shoes. They walked back to the stall, red water still pouring out from under the wooden doorway.

"Take out your guns," Axel whispered.

"What?" asked Taggart.

"Taggart, Billie, just take out your guns."

As if to placate a fussy kid, the two cops pulled their guns out of their holsters. Billie looked proudly at his weapon. It was the first time it had left its snug leather nest—except, of course, when he practiced his draw at home in front of the mirror.

Axel swung open the stable door. Inside was an elderly man wearing Empyrean Fields overalls. He had a hose in one hand and a brush in the other. He sang softly in Spanish to a beautiful gray as he hosed red mud off the horse's flanks and legs.

Axel sounded scared. "Where has this horse been?"

The man half turned. His eyes widened as he saw Axel and the guns pointed at him. One of the guns was bigger than the hose he had in his hands and the man who held it had the eyes of a cold-blooded killer.

"Where has this horse been?" asked Axel, more urgently this time.

"Grazing," he said, thinking a prayer, "in the pasture."

"And where is the pasture?"

"Madre de Dios," said the unhappy groom.

"Tell me," said Axel, pretending to panic, "or they'll kill us both."

The elderly groom didn't falter. "Up there," he said, pointing toward the wall. "Up there in the hills. In Mr. Dent's oil field."

Taggart knew there were a hundred different sets of hills in this part of the world. "What hills?" he demanded fiercely. "What are they called?"

"Baldwin Hills Park," said the man. "Baldwin Hills Park, where all Mr. Dent's horses go to pasture."

"Let's go," ordered Rosewood.

"Thanks, man," said Axel. "Yours might be the last friendly face I see." Axel followed the other two out of the stable. As soon as they were gone, the elderly groom fell to his knees in the muddy water and gave fervent thanks to all his favorite saints for the sparing of his life. He felt bad about the black guy, so he said a few prayers for him too.

The Plymouth zoomed up into the hills, Rosewood behind the wheel. Axel filled the other two in.

"Bogomil had red mud all over his jogging shoes. My hunch is that he got some kind of tip about this Baldwin Hills place, checked it out, and they tried to waste him."

"But the robberies, the hit at Adriano's, Cal Deposit. Dent doesn't need the money."

"That's where you're wrong, Taggart. Dent's going broke. He arranges some good hits to get some operating capital, makes up some phony codes that keep us guessing until he wants us to know that Cain is the 'mastermind' behind the whole thing. Frame Cain. Kill Cain. Case closed. Dent's home free."

Rosewood shook his head. He still didn't get it. "But why would an oilman risk all this to transport oil-field equipment to Costa Rica? Even if he's down on his luck, he could've gotten a loan or something."

The landscape was changing. Just as Bogomil had noticed, they had left the plush homes behind and were in hilly country. It was hard to believe that there was a city within a hundred miles of them—except for the fact that every few seconds an airliner flew low over them in the dusk, landing carriage down, brake flaps up.

"There an airport around here?" asked Axel.

"Yeah," said Taggart, thinking for once that Axel didn't know everything. "It's called LAX."

"Hey, Axel," said Rosewood, "answer my question."

"What was it, Billie? I forgot it already."

"The oil equipment. You're telling me Dent would rob and kill to protect it?"

Axel sighed. His pupil just wasn't catching on. "Billie, Dent's not buying oil equipment."

"But you saw . . ."

"What it said on those lists and what is actually going on are two different things."

"C'mon," said Taggart, "tell me he's *exporting* drugs to Central America. That would certainly be a switch."

"No, not drugs," said Axel patiently. "I'll bet he's buying guns from Thomopolis. Then he's selling them through one of his old contacts in Central America."

"But the racetrack . . ."

"He steals his own money—pays it to Thomopolis, and then gets it back from insurance." *Nice and neat,* thought Axel. Except he planned on making things a little messy for old Max Dent.

"But why isn't Dent just splitting with all the money he stole?" asked a still-bewildered Rosewood.

"First of all, Billie, he paid it all to Thomopolis. Second, why be content with a couple of million when you can have ten or twenty? The oil business—it comes and it goes. But guns, the price is always high for guns. People who can't get them legally will pay any price. A million spent on guns up here turns into ten million down there. Get it?"

Finally, Rosewood got it. "Ohhh, I see."

"Good," said Axel. "Stop the car."

Rosewood skidded to a stop. They looked out over the hills, the grazing horses, and the oil pumps, which worked the precious liquid out of the ground.

"Look at all that oil," whispered Taggart in awe.

"I don't see any oil," said Axel.

"What? You blind? Don't you see the—"

"I see trucks," said Axel grimly. He pointed across the valley to a distant hillside. There were two large trucks heading up a dirt track on the far hill, making for the single oil tank that Bogomil had looked at with such suspicion. In the late afternoon sunlight, they could make out a guard perched on the holding-tank ladder, his silhouette—rifle included—thrown into sharp relief by the rays of the setting sun.

"I think we better go over there and make sure he's got a permit for that weapon," said Axel.

They started down the slope into the shallow valley, guns drawn. All three were aware that they were running straight into the sun and that the guard need only glance their way to see them. They did their best to keep under cover, zigzagging from rocks to trees to oil pumps in an effort not to be seen.

It took them twenty minutes to cross five hundred yards of open ground. Finally, though, they were against the gas tank, on the side opposite to the guard. And he still hadn't seen them. Silently, Axel motioned Taggart and Rosewood to work their way around the tank toward the thug while Axel went the other way. Taggart nodded and led the way.

Axel inched along the side of the tank. The metal was warm against his skin. He had to be quiet; he wanted the guard taken out silently. Axel had a pretty good idea that those trucks he had seen would have a fair number of Dent's goons in them. He didn't want the shooting to start unless Axel had surprise on his side. He, Rosewood, and Taggart were tremendously outnumbered; from what Axel had seen of Karla's shooting, he didn't doubt that she alone would be pretty tough to bring down, so Axel wanted all of the surprise to be working for him.

The guard certainly was surprised when he came face-to-face with Axel. Axel fixed a big grin on him.

"Hi," he said, sounding as sincere as a door-to-door salesman, "have you ever asked yourself why Jesus permits evil in the world?"

If the question had ever occurred to the brawny guy, he didn't show it. He *was* asking himself, however, why the Bible salesman was holding a Browning 9mm automatic. But that was all he managed to think. From behind, Taggart clubbed the guy with the handle of his .38. It was a blow strong enough to put a dent even in the guard's thick skull.

He slumped against the oil tank, making the container boom dully, and then slid to the ground.

Axel looked down at the red mud they now all had on their shoes. "This is it. Bogomil was up here."

"And look at this, Axel," said Rosewood. He had stuck his finger in a two-inch-wide hole in the tank. "Seems to me that if there was oil in this thing, it would be leaking out."

"That isn't Billie Rosewood, friend of plants, animals, and large-caliber weapons," said Axel to Taggart. "This here is Sherlock Holmes."

Axel stuck his finger in the hole too, felt around, and then pulled it out. There wasn't so much as an oil stain on it. "This tank never held oil," he said. "Let's take a look on top." He climbed to the top of the tank. The valve in the center of the oil tank's roof was frozen shut with rust. Axel nodded to himself and then started down the ladder. Halfway to the ground he saw that one of the steel plates was loose.

"Billie, you still got that carving knife on you?"

Billie reached into an inside pocket and handed the switchblade up to Axel. The knife flicked open noiselessly and Axel jammed the strong blade under the loose sheet of steel. There was the sound of tearing metal, and a simple lock pulled away from its moorings inside the tank. The sheet was nothing more than a badly concealed secret door. It swung inward and Axel peered in.

It took a moment for his eyes to adjust to the darkness, but once they had cleared, he saw what appeared to be a fairly large, well-equipped carpenter's shop. There was a portable generator connected to a number of machine tools: a table saw, a bandsaw, a belt sander. There were stacks of lumber laid across sawhorses, the floor of the tank an inch deep in sawdust. He suddenly fixed his eyes on what had been made here. Stacked in a corner was a neat pile of boxes. Directly below him, sitting on top of a pile of unused lumber, was a shipping label. Axel reached as far as he could and managed to grab the piece of paper. It read: "Oil-field Parts."

"If these are oil-field parts," he said aloud, "I'm a waltzing mouse."

"A what, Axel?" Rosewood called from behind him on the ladder.

"Never mind, Billie." Axel sat on the edge of the tank and then dropped into the room. Billie's face appeared where Axel had been a moment before. After a second's hesitation, he followed Axel into the tank. Axel looked around him a moment, then stripped a tarp off one of the larger boxes. There, packed in grease and straw, were brand-new Valmet automatic rifles. Axel guessed there were a hundred, maybe a hundred and fifty of them in the case. He could see now that the rest of the tank was full of boxes as large or larger than that one. The entire oil tank was an armory and the goods were stacked there as if on a loading dock.

Axel nodded, as if confirming something to himself. Dent would probably keep a stock here safe and sound in the United States and send for it as he needed it, the stuff always going out as oil parts. After all, wasn't Maxwell Dent a respected oilman?

Billie ripped the tarp off another box. He picked up what appeared to be a brick made out of modeling clay and wrapped in heavy oiled paper. He gingerly put it down. He knew plastic explosive when he saw it.

Axel had found another case of rifles. "See, Billie, in poor countries, where this shit is going, they drill for oil by firing high-powered rifles directly into the ground. That's why they're so poor."

They pried open a number of other boxes. "This shit is unbelievable," said Axel in awe. Like any cop, he hated to see guns fall into the wrong hands, but this went way beyond guns. They found mortars,

M-79 grenade launchers, R-P handheld rocket launchers—coincidentally, Axel noted, made in the USSR—Steyr AKMs, the western copy of the AK-47; AUGs, which were perfect jungle-warfare guns. There were crates of ammunition to match all of them. In the last case they opened, they found thousands of hand grenades.

Like a kid choosing a piece of chocolate from a giant selection, Axel gingerly picked up one of the grenades and jammed it into his pocket. It looked like he had stuffed a grapefruit there.

"Time to catch the bad guys," he said, singsong, as he put a ladder against the wall beneath the opening of the tank. Rosewood climbed out, followed closely by Axel. As he put his foot on the bottom rung of the ladder, he noticed a shotgun leaning against the wall, a belt of shells wound around it. *Nice and old-fashioned,* he thought as he grabbed it and climbed out into the light.

"So?" said Taggart. "What's in there?"

"Weapons," said Axel. "Enough to start and win a war."

They huddled at the base of the tank. "So?" said Axel. "Want to take them?"

"I think we're going to have to, Axel," said Taggart soberly.

"Just the three of us?"

"We'll get it started," said Taggart, "and hope that help shows up."

"What's the rush?" asked Rosewood.

Taggart shrugged. "While you were in there"—he jabbed a thumb at the tank—"I went along aways and saw Dent and that broad and Thomopolis in the distance. They have some guys—twenty maybe—loading up the trucks with stuff from a hut up there."

"Yeah?"

"They also have a chopper."

"So?" asked Billie. "What is it, a Huey gunship?"

"No," said Taggart, "a nice little executive model. The kind you fly into LAX just in time to catch your flight."

"So as soon as the trucks are loaded . . ." said Axel.

"Everybody is out of here," finished Rosewood.

"And we couldn't catch them," said Axel. "Not even with Billie behind the wheel."

Rosewood grinned.

"Okay, I say now," said Axel.

"Me too," said Billie.

Taggart nodded. He was in.

Axel grinned. "Well *finally,* guys, one for all, all for one, and all that shit."

"Right," said Taggart.

Axel turned to Rosewood. "Okay, Billie, here's what you do. I want you to go back the way we came. Get on the radio and put out a call—officer down, shots fired. After that, get your ass back here. We're gonna need your help." Billie got to one knee and started off, but Axel grabbed him by the sleeve. "And Billie," he said soberly, "what happens from now on isn't a game. It's gonna get very scary, so cover your ass."

Rosewood nodded grimly and set off, darting back the way they had come, keeping his head down, his heart pounding.

Thomopolis's giant Rolls Royce was facing down

the road. The car alone was worth close to two hundred thousand dollars. That meant you could buy fifty more of the elegant automobiles with the ten million dollars that was packed in several suitcases in the trunk. It was the payoff from Dent.

Dent, Karla, and Thomopolis toasted each other with champagne that one of Thomopolis's thugs had dug out of the little refrigerator in the back of the Rolls. Taggart and Axel had crawled up close enough to the hut to hear what the three were talking about.

"What time does your plane leave?" asked Thomopolis. He would be much happier with Dent out of the country. Of course, at this late stage, what could possibly go wrong?

Dent glanced at his watch. "We're just a few minutes from the airport," he said as he watched his luggage and Karla's being loaded into the helicopter. "There is no rush. You and your men can go whenever you're ready."

Axel could just make out one of Karla's long legs. He never did get to give her that shave . . . Too bad.

"Did you notify Costa Rica that we'll be coming in tonight?" Dent asked her.

She smiled languorously and stretched like a cat. "They told me that there will be champagne chilling when we arrive."

It's going to be warm and flat by the time you get there, said Axel to himself. He tapped Taggart on the shoulder and silently they backed away from the hut. They went around the building and watched loaders carrying heavy boxes and placing them on the back of one of the trucks. They would probably leave

LAX sometime that night. Plenty of time to pick them up later, Axel decided. The bearers were being watched by one of the drivers, who seemed to be some kind of foreman. He was just leaning against the vehicle, not moving a muscle to help.

"Taggart," hissed Axel, "you got a pen?"

Taggart patted his pockets. "What the hell are you going to do? Write a letter?"

"Right first time," said Axel, taking the pen from him. He quickly scribbled a note on the back of the packing label he had taken from the tank. He checked the note carefully and then turned to Taggart.

"Stay here."

"Axel?" demanded Taggart. "Where the hell are you going?"

"To deliver the message, man," said Axel, walking boldly out from his cover. Taggart watched him go and shook his head. Although he did notice that for the first time in days, the pain in his arm was gone.

The driver was startled when Axel appeared, but he assumed the black guy was working for Dent or the Greek or else he never would have made it onto the property.

"What the hell do you want?"

"For Maxwell Dent. We got trouble with the other tank. Very important."

"Why the fuck don't you give it to him? I'm a driver."

"Well, I'm in a fuckin' hurry," said Axel. "But if Dent doesn't get this, it's your ass, not mine."

Axel headed back down the hill. The driver

looked at the note and then heaved himself off the truck, tossed away the cigarette he was smoking, and walked toward the boss.

"It has been a pleasure, Nikos," said Dent, shaking hands with Thomopolis. "And I'm sure we shall be doing more business in the future."

"I certainly hope so," said Nikos, taking Dent's thin hand in his own hairy paw. "The next time with a little less . . . unpleasantness, I hope." He meant, of course, no more crimes like Adriano's or the shooting of Bogomil—no crime, in fact, that couldn't be committed with a computer and a telex machine.

"Naturally not." Dent laughed. "I am an established dealer in . . . machinery now."

"As long as you remain a client and not a competitor"—Thomopolis laughed—"I shall be happy."

Dent smiled thinly. Already he had heard of a load of FN automatic rifles available in Algeria that he could have at half the price Nikos would have charged. "I shall be a *faithful* client."

"Good." Thomopolis turned to Karla. "Miss Fry, it has been a great pleasure." Karla's hand disappeared under the mustache as Nikos bent to kiss it.

"Good-bye, Mr. Thomopolis," she said, wishing she could extract her hand.

The truck driver had handed Dent the note. Karla noticed. Thomopolis noticed.

Ashen, Dent turned to the driver. "Who gave you this?"

"Some guy, Mr. Dent."

"Some guy! No one you recognized?"

"Not bad news, I hope," said Thomopolis.

The note was written in the simple, number runner's code that Axel had learned a long time ago on the streets of Detroit. Dent translated it quickly. It didn't say much, but it spoke volumes. It meant that Foley was on to them; it meant that right at that moment, Dent's carefully planned venture was coming unstuck. Worst of all, it meant that Foley was somewhere around.

"What does it say?" demanded Karla.

"You are . . ." he began in a normal tone of voice. Then Dent roared. *"Shit out of luck F-O-L-E-Y."* He scowled at Karla. "Son-of-a-bitch!"

Karla smiled softly. Getting Foley would be the best part of this operation. She had vowed to get him, and now, at the last minute, she had been given the chance.

"Foley?" asked Thomopolis. "Who is this Foley?"

"The asshole at the party, the one at the Playboy Mansion."

Thomopolis's heavy features darkened. He had been made a fool of by that man, and Nikos Thomopolis didn't like that sort of thing. He barked out a few orders to his goons, who came running to him double speed for such heavy guys. Thomopolis gave them instructions in Greek. They nodded and hauled their guns out from beneath their coats.

Karla appeared from within the hut clutching a machine pistol. She tossed it to Dent, who took out the clip and checked to see that it was full; he spun it around to look at the second magazine that had been taped to the side of the first. He was ready.

Karla wrapped a holster belt around her slim waist

and pulled out the big Dan Wesson .357. She was secretly excited. She had thought her shooting days were over. She jammed a dozen big shells into the pocket of her leather jumpsuit. She and Dent took off, looking for cover. Looking for Axel.

Axel and Taggart watched all this from behind an oil pump.

"Well," said Axel with a grin, "you ready for the battle of Beverly Hills?"

"I got a choice?" asked Taggart. But he was smiling.

CHAPTER
FOURTEEN

The battle of Beverly Hills began, predictably enough, with a bang. A big one—and Axel was responsible for it. He and Taggart moved away from the hut and hid behind a couple of boulders, waiting for the enemy to come over the rise at them. Axel decided he'd start things off in grand fashion. He pulled the pin from the single grenade he had stolen from the phony oil tank.

A startled Taggart watched as Axel dashed a few yards toward the tank and tossed the bomb through the open door. Taggart wished he had had time to dig himself a nice deep hole. Instead, he buried his face in the damp earth and kept his ass down. Axel came racing back, diving behind the rock for cover. Then he heard Rosewood's voice. Axel glanced up and saw Billie standing as tall as a flagpole, totally unaware that a half ton of explosives and ammunition was about to blow up unnervingly close at hand.

"What's next, guys?" he asked casually. Axel reached up and grabbed Billie by the belt, yanking him to the ground.

"Cover up, Billie!" screamed Axel.

"Why?"

Axel didn't bother to explain, he just pushed Rosewood into the mud, muffling Rosewood's questions.

Thomopolis, Dent, Karla, and a half-dozen body-guards were cresting the hill just as the tank blew.

It wasn't one explosion or two but dozens, one coming on top of another. Tremendous booms rolled down the valley toward Beverly Hills—they could be heard in Santa Monica miles away. A fountain of fire shot into the sky. Axel could feel the heat of it on his back. Residents in the area cursed their realtors: they had bought houses half a mile from an erupting volcano.

The force of the first explosion knocked Dent and his crowd flat. As one of his gunmen staggered to his feet, he was immediately cut down by a bullet—it hadn't been fired by Axel, Taggart or Rosewood. It was one of the millions of rounds of ammunition that had been detonated by the explosion. The bullets, all types and all calibers, crackled like firecrackers, short sharp cracks that played counterpoint to the more dramatic, thundering explosions. The tank sides were peppered with shells and they sprayed out through the thin sides, ricocheting all over the hillside.

There was a third, more terrifying sound in that lonely place. The horses, who had been grazing peacefully until a few seconds before, were terrified by the blast. They immediately started stampeding, screaming in fear, running frenzied from the sound. A couple of the creatures were creased by the bullets that seemed to fill the air. The horses plunged and reared, bit and kicked in an effort to get away. In a matter of seconds the pounding hooves had churned the hillside into a sea of red mud and broken turf.

"Shit," Axel mumbled into the ground, "and we haven't even started shooting yet."

He didn't have long to wait. He peered over the top of his boulder. Thomopolis saw him and his goons let rip with their weapons, chipping a few inches of rock off the top of the boulder. Stone fragments whipped through the air around them and the whine of bullets zoomed by their ears.

Rosewood wanted to say, "We're pinned down, men," the way they did in the movies, but he was afraid that Taggart would think he had lost his mind. Also, there was hardly any reason to point that out to Axel and Taggart. They were perfectly aware of the predicament they were in.

Axel chanced a glimpse over the top of the rock, and in that split second he saw that Dent and Karla had left the fight to Thomopolis and his thugs. They were racing toward the chopper. They were getting the hell out. Obviously the explosion was going to attract every cop in the southern part of the state. The hell with getting Foley—the time to leave was at hand.

But Axel had other plans.

"Taggart! Billie! Can you cover me?"

"We can try," said Taggart, grim-faced.

"Good." Axel darted left from behind the rocks and immediately Thomopolis's men started shooting at him. He zigzagged across a piece of open ground, saying every prayer he knew, all at the same time. As soon as Axel left the sheltering rocks, Taggart jumped to his feet, his .38 spewing bullets at the men on the ridge. One of them grunted and spun away, falling to the ground. He didn't move.

Taggart didn't see one of the Greek's goons on the far left of the ridge. The man took careful aim at Taggart's ear . . .

The thunderclap that erupted next to Taggart made him dive for cover. He was sure that someone had tossed a grenade at them. Instead, he looked up and saw Rosewood, his giant .44 smoking in his hand. All that remained of the guy who was going to drill Taggart were some wisps and tatters of a very expensive suit.

Billie flopped down next to Taggart. He grinned. "I got one. Did you see that?" Pride filled his voice.

Hot lead was ripping up their position as the gunmen poured bullets at the boulders.

"I'll never smoke another cigar again," said Taggart to God, "if You promise that Billie never does that again."

Billie grinned and thumbed back the hammer on his cannon. "Let's give them some more covering fire. That's what they're supposed to be doing, right?"

Like cobras rearing up from behind a rock, Taggart and Rosewood stood up, their guns blasting. They emptied their clips, the goons diving for cover at this sudden and unexpected display of firepower.

As if they were controlled by the same set of circuits, Rosewood and Taggart went down again to reload. Taggart tensed and stopped loading.

"Sarge? What's the matter?" Rosewood was afraid that a stray round had hit Taggart.

"Sshh, listen."

Rosewood lay stock-still and listened. Then he grinned broadly. Another sound had been added to the din, this one more welcome. The air was filled with the sound of sirens, hundreds of them. Police cars were racing up the twisting streets into the hills.

"The cavalry," said Rosewood delightedly. He jammed at the cylinder of his .44 full of giant slugs, stood up, and blazed away at the gunmen as if he were impervious to lead. Taggart shook his head and guessed that it would be safe for him to start smoking cigars again without bringing down the wrath of God. He flung himself up and started blasting in unison with Billie. *Of course,* Taggart wondered, *how much worse could God's anger be than this firefight?*

Panting with exertion and the adrenaline pumping through his body, Axel had made it to the little hut that had served as Dent's headquarters on the hill. Once inside, he realized that it was a stable, a warren of little rooms and stalls. His shotgun held out in front of him, Axel moved cautiously from room to room. Karla and Dent were in here somewhere. . . .

He nudged open a door with the snout of the shotgun, the old wood creaking on its hinges. Despite the world war and stampede that was going on outside, it was curiously quiet in the stuffy building. Axel's breathing seemed loud and he was sure that the beating of his heart could be heard three hundred yards away.

Suddenly, the wall next to Axel exploded. He threw himself away from the blast and caught a glimpse of Karla, firing away at him with her magnum. Instinctively, he pulled both triggers of his shotgun, the cartridges splintering a stall door. But Karla wasn't there.

Axel was flat on the cement floor. He broke the shotgun and slipped two more cartridges into the breech. With a satisfying snap, he closed the gun. *That was pretty rotten shooting,* he reflected, *for a woman like Karla. She must be nervous. She had a clear shot and she blew it.*

That was about all the time Axel had for thinking. Dent appeared out of nowhere. He was carrying a machine pistol and he had a determined look in his eyes. The machine pistol chattered, shredding the floor and walls where Axel had been just a second before. He dove for a group of rusting oil drums and found some cover there as the bullets splattered around him. Axel blasted both barrels of his shotgun.

"Get the fuck off my back!" he yelled at Dent as the twin-barreled gun sprayed shot all over the room. He peered over the top of one of the tanks, hoping he would see Dent dead on the floor. But he was disappointed. There was no sign of Dent or Karla. The front door of the ramshackle shack swung on its hinges. From outside, Axel heard the low whine of the chopper engine starting up.

Axel rolled out of his cover, dashed outside, and dove to his right to avoid being cut down in any covering fire that Karla might be providing. But there wasn't any. She was getting into the helicopter with her boss. Dust kicked up as the rotors started turning slowly.

Axel was dimly aware of the sound of sirens in the

air. But he had other things on his mind. He jumped into the payload of one of the half-loaded trucks and kicked open one of the boxes. He hit pay dirt with the first crate. There were a dozen M-79 grenade launchers wrapped in packing. Axel tore one from the box, loaded it, and drew a bead on the chopper that was just lifting off the ground. Axel wanted to put the grenade right in the glass-enclosed cockpit. But even Axel wasn't very familiar with a grenade launcher. They didn't use them much, not even in Detroit.

But he blasted away the best he could. The grenade missed the cockpit but the bomb clipped the edge of one of the rotors. The engine screamed and blew out, the chopper dipping, faltering, and falling crazily to earth. For one brief moment, he saw the chopper whole on the ground, and then the fuel tank exploded on contact, throwing up a sheet of flame. Axel threw himself to the ground as the chopper came crashing down, crawling under the truck to avoid the flames and the still-swirling rotors that chopped the two-and-a-half-ton truck to shreds.

When Axel dared look out from his cover, the chopper was lying broken on its side, burning furiously. He caught a glimpse of Dent running away from the destroyed chopper. The man appeared to have as many lives as Axel did.

Dent threw himself behind an oil pump, his machine pistol still in his hand. He had decided that even if he only had a few minutes to live, he was going to take that Axel Foley with him. He cocked the gun and waited for his chance. A sharp pain was coursing up his leg. He had been hit by something, but that didn't matter anymore. Foley. He wanted Foley.

Axel had jammed two more cartridges into his shotgun and ducked back around the hut. He sprinted across some open ground, noticing as he went that some B.H.P.D. uniforms were shooting it out with Thomopolis and his goons. That didn't interest him. He wanted Dent, and when he got him, he was going after Karla, wherever the hell she was.

Someone squeezed off a round at him and he dove for cover. He wasn't sure if he had been shot at by the police, the Greek, or Dent. Axel scanned the open ground, looking for Dent. He found him behind the oil pump, catching a glimpse of him as the pump head moved up. For a second, Dent was obscured as the pump came down again. Axel timed his movements to the pump. As soon as the weight had dropped in front of Dent, Axel dashed around to Dent's left. A few seconds later he was standing behind the would-be arms dealer, his shotgun aimed at Dent's head.

But it wasn't in Axel to blow a man away from behind like that. He sighed. This was going to have to be a plain old-fashioned bust. Let the courts figure it out . . .

"Okay, Max," said Axel quietly, "you've had your fun, but you are out of business."

Axel really did expect Dent to realize he had been beaten. After all, there was a cop standing behind him with a shotgun aimed at his heart. Who would be stupid enough to try and roll over and drop Axel with a machine pistol? It just couldn't be done. Well, Max Dent thought he had a chance.

Dent flopped over like a fish, his finger yanking the trigger, sending a few rounds Axel's way.

If that's the way you want to play, thought Axel. Both barrels of the shotgun roared and Axel blew Maxwell Dent to hell. Axel sighed. That was too much like an execution for his taste.

He didn't even bother to reload. The uniforms were mopping up the Greek's gang, and he figured Karla must have been killed in the crash of the chopper. He hadn't seen those legs around in the last couple minutes. It was all over.

But it wasn't. As Axel stood over Dent's broken body, he felt the hot barrel of a gun pressed against his neck.

He tensed, but realized that his weapon was unloaded. There wasn't a damn thing he could do.

Axel smelled the perfume and knew exactly who stood behind, ready to kill him.

"Look's like this is good-bye, Axel," said Karla breathily.

"Karla, I know there is very little I can say to change your mind . . ."

"There is nothing you can say," she spat. Axel heard the hammer of her .357 cock. In his ear it sounded louder than the explosion he had set off thirty minutes earlier.

"Karla," said Axel, "killing a cop, that's a serious—"

But his words were lost in the roar of a gun firing. It felt like it was inside his head. For a split second, Axel was sure he was dead. Then he saw a wave of blond hair at his feet. He looked around. Karla was sprawled in the muddy earth, her perfectly manicured finger still on the trigger of her gun. Blood was soaking the side of her head. Axel looked up and saw Taggart, grim-faced, his gun smoking.

There must have been a couple of hundred policemen on the scene now. The lights flashed on top of the marked units. Radio chatter filled the air. A convoy of ambulances came screaming up the rough roads. Nikos Thomopolis was demanding that he speak to his attorney. Horses, still spooked by all the gunplay, ran this way and that whinnying in distress.

As if someone had pulled a plug, Axel felt the tension draining from him. The Alphabet bandits were no more, the shooting of his friend Andrew Bogomil avenged.

The battle of Beverly Hills was over. And the good guys had won.

Axel wondered how he was going to explain all this to Inspector Todd.

CHAPTER
FIFTEEN

Or, for that matter, how he was going to explain all this to Chief Lutz. The last time Axel, Rosewood, and Taggart had started a firefight in Beverly Hills, they had had Captain Bogomil to go to bat for them—to explain things to the old chief, to smooth things over with Todd. This time it was just the three of them; two traffic cops and a Detroit detective had to explain to Lutz why they had solved crimes that had already been "solved"—and why they had blown away one of Beverly Hills' richest and most respected businessmen, the late Maxwell Dent, not to mention his assistant, Karla Fry.

But nothing in Beverly Hills ever happens quite the way you expect it to. Help in explaining this mess arrived from the strangest place. It was Nikos Thomopolis who helped them out of the jam they were in. He demanded, and he was allowed, to see his attorney. It was his lawyer who convinced the arms dealer to turn state's evidence and confirm everything Axel, Taggart, and Rosewood had said. If he did that, Thomopolis's attorney had said, he could guarantee Nikos a fine, a few dozen weekends in the slammer, and a couple of hundred hours of community service. If Thomopolis insisted that he was innocent, the lawyer said the best he could do was seven to nine in Joliet.

Thomopolis decided that he would sing.

And the best part about Nikos Thomopolis's unexpected help was that he wasn't confessing to a police department headed by Chief Harold Lutz. Mayor Egan—the man that Lutz had long since recognized as the political power in Beverly Hills, the man who had the power to hire and fire—had exercised his power. He had fired Chief Lutz and immediately placed Andrew Bogomil in his position.

Bogomil had gone into the intensive care unit a captain. When he woke up a few days later, blissfully unaware of the havoc that Axel Foley had wrought on his behalf for the past seventy-two hours, his daughter Jan and the mayor were at his bedside to tell him of his rise in status and fortune.

Bogomil had had only one question. "Has Axel been out here?"

Tears of happiness sprang into Jan's eyes. Her father was back, alive, well, and smart enough to realize that Axel Foley must have had a hand in tracking down the Alphabet bandit.

Taggart picked Axel up at the Rosenberg mansion the morning after the shoot-out and filled him in on what had happened in the last twelve hours. They swung by Rosewood's apartment and all three of them drove to the headquarters of the Beverly Hills Police Department.

Axel was pleased for his friends. But he still faced the problem of what he was going to do about his own position in Detroit. But he didn't mention it. He had done what he had planned to do and that was enough, for the time being.

It was Taggart who took the load off of Axel's mind. As they pushed open the doors of headquarters and walked past the booking desk, Taggart acted as if something that had slipped his mind had suddenly come back to him.

"Oh yeah," said Taggart, "and another thing . . ."

"Another thing?" asked Axel.

"Our mayor has been talking to your mayor all morning," Taggart said.

Axel stopped. "What do you mean, man, *your* mayor. *My* mayor. I don't have a mayor. I got an inspector."

"The way I hear it," said Rosewood, butting in, "Mayor Egan of Beverly Hills has been talking to the mayor of Detroit, trying to get you your job back."

"No shit," said Axel. "How did he do?"

"Uh, I don't know."

"But there's hope, right?"

"Definitely," said Taggart, as if he meant it.

As they walked down the hall toward the chief's office, they met Lutz coming toward them. His arms were filled with papers, plaques, and other personal effects from his office. Biddle was behind him, pushing a wheeled office chair piled high with more of Lutz's belongings.

"What?" said Axel. "Lutz fucks up the whole thing and he gets rewarded with a bigger office?"

"That's something else," whispered Rosewood. "We got a new chief."

"Lutz is out?"

"History," said Taggart happily.

Axel was face-to-face with Lutz now. "Hey, Harold," he said, "I hear you're out of a job."

Lutz stopped in the hallway and sneered at Axel. "I may not be the only one, Foley."

"Yeah," said Axel, "but I'm young and brilliant and handsome." He smoothed his hand over the top of his head. "I'll get my job back, and if I do, I could use a good undercover cop back in Detroit."

"You could, huh?"

"Yeah. Listen, Harold, would you be willing to dress up as a woman?"

"Very funny," said Lutz sourly. "Now get out of my way." Lutz brushed past him, the ever-loyal Biddle following. As they disappeared down the hall, Axel could hear Biddle pleading with Lutz: "The least you could have done was listen to him. Detroit isn't such a bad town . . . and a lot of cops do decoy work in drag."

"Shut up, Biddle."

"So," said Axel, turning to Rosewood and Taggart, "who's the new chief? Let me guess, Frank Sinatra. Am I right? Tell me I'm right."

"You're wrong," said Taggart happily. "He wants to see you."

Sitting behind Lutz's old desk was Andrew Bogomil. He was still dressed in hospital clothing and was in a wheelchair, but he looked good. There was no doubt he was on the mend. He beamed at Axel.

"Andrew!" said Axel. "You lost weight!"

"Sssh," said Bogomil, putting a finger to his lips, "you'll disturb the mayor." Egan was sitting on the couch talking on the phone. "He's talking to someone who might play a major role in your future."

"So," said Axel, dropping into one of the chairs in front of Bogomil's new desk. "Tell me, Andrew, think you'll ever make chief?"

"I made it, Axel," said Bogomil with a laugh. "You should try going into a coma for a few days. You might wake up commander."

Egan put his hand over the phone. "You might have made it anyway, Detective Foley. I'm talking to your boss, an Inspector Todd."

"Todd . . ." said Axel. He could imagine that Mayor Egan was learning words that he didn't know existed. Axel figured he had better start looking for a job right then, and what better place to start than with his old pal Bogomil. After all, he'd had a sudden rise in the world.

"I *am* talking to the chief of the Beverly Hills Police Department," said Axel.

"That's right," said Bogomil with a smile. "Be careful . . . what you say could be held against you."

"Everything else has been," said Axel.

Bogomil held out his hand and Axel shook it. "I'll never be able to tell you how grateful I am, Axel."

"Well, Andrew, there is something you could do. Now that you are the chief of this department and everything, and I'm out of a job . . ."

Bogomil paled slightly. Was Beverly Hills ready for Axel Foley full-time? Andrew didn't think so. Luckily, the mayor came to his rescue.

Egan had been listening with one ear to what Axel

was asking of the new chief of police. The mayor raised his voice. "Well, Inspector, as I told your mayor, I want you to know how thankful we are that you allowed Foley the time to help us with this case. He's quite a detective."

"I did *what?*" Todd bellowed. "Foley is quite a *what?*" Todd grumbled a number of things about Foley that made Mayor Egan go red in the face.

"Well," said Egan, "that is certainly a"—he groped for the right word—"colorful way of putting it."

"Colorful?" roared Todd. "That son-of-a-bitch is an insubordinate . . ."

"Axel has told us, Inspector Todd, that everything he knows he learned under your expert tutelage."

"My *what?*" Todd yelled. "Listen. Is Foley there?"

"Yes he is," said Egan.

"Lemme talk to him."

Axel took the phone as if it were a time bomb that no one on the bomb squad had figured out how to defuse yet. "Hi, Inspector," he said, sounding as cheerful as he could.

Todd, as usual, wanted to talk to Axel, but, again as usual, he wasn't happy to hear his voice. The inspector glanced over at Jeffrey Friedman, who was sitting in the only other chair in Todd's office, his right leg in a heavy cast.

"Axel? What the fuck is expert tutelage? And what the fuck are you doing saying you learned it under mine?"

"It doesn't mean anything, really, boss," said

Axel. Despite himself, he was glad to hear Todd yelling at him. It was the way things were supposed to be. The way the universe was ordered; if Todd ever stopped yelling at him, Axel was afraid that the polar ice caps would melt or that the planet Saturn would fly out of its orbit and hit Indiana. Suddenly Axel was very homesick for Detroit, for the shitty detective squad room, and for criminals who acted like criminals. "People just talk funny in California, Inspector. I think it has something to do with the ocean."

Todd shook his head. "I don't know how you do it, Foley. Yesterday I fired your ass. But today, the mayor of Detroit wants to give me a special commendation for lending your services to the Beverly Hills Police Department."

"I'd certainly say you deserved that, sir," said Axel soberly.

Todd ignored him. "And two other things, Foley. Number one, your secret undercover partner Friedman wrecked the Ferrari, and when he did, he had it full of ugly broads."

"Axel!" yelled Jeffrey, hoping to make himself heard over Todd's voice. "Axel, that was Beverly, my fiancée, and her mother."

"Wrecked the Ferrari," moaned Axel. "Jeffrey, how could you?"

"Fuck the Ferrari," roared Todd. "The other thing is that now you're done being a California hero, I want you to put your skinny ass on fast forward and come here and be a Michigan hero. You were supposed to solve me an undercover case two days ago."

Axel grinned into the phone. *Come home, Axel,* Todd was saying, *all is forgiven.* "I'll be there, Inspector."

"Good," said Todd, and hung up.

Axel went back to his stolen house to pack up his few belongings. Taggart and Rosewood waited outside; they had been detailed by Chief Bogomil to drive him to the airport. He came down the long driveway of the mansion, looking back at the house wistfully. He had a feeling it would be a while before he had as nice a place as that to live in again.

"You really going home, Axel?" asked Rosewood. "Seems to me you deserve a vacation."

"No, Billie, you guys wear me out. Getting back to some nice mid-American urban street violence— that'll be a vacation."

Taggart put out his hand. Axel took it in both of his and shook it warmly. "Listen, Taggart," he said, "I got some women for you to meet in Detroit."

"Axel . . ." said Taggart, blushing.

"No really, there are a lot of good women who'd love to boil your laundry, cook, oil your .38, and all that shit."

Taggart looked away, embarrassed.

"Maureen came back," interjected Rosewood.

"Taggart, you *stud!*" Axel laughed. "She couldn't live without you!"

Taggart scuffed his shoes in the dirt. "Nah, it's just that her mother didn't have cable TV."

Axel laughed as he tossed his bag in the back of his giant black El Dorado. He opened the door.

"Hey," said Rosewood, "we're supposed to drive you to the airport."

"No," said Axel, "I'd rather do it myself. Drop off the car. I hate good-byes, you know how it is. . . ." A long, sleek Rolls Royce limo was slowing down in front of the house. Axel's eyes narrowed. He had a feeling he knew who was in the car.

Axel got behind the wheel of his Caddy and started the engine.

Rosewood clapped him on the shoulder. "Thanks, Axel," he said.

"Take care of yourself, Billie." Axel slipped the car into gear, but held his foot on the brake. He noticed that an elderly couple was being assisted from the Rolls by a chauffeur. They were looking up at the house, surprised that the work had not been finished.

Taggart stepped forward. "Anything we can do for you, Axel?"

Axel gunned the engine. "Well, there is one thing . . ."

"Name it," said Taggart, feeling expansive. "It's done."

Axel put the keys of the house in Taggart's hand. He gestured over his shoulder at the shocked faces of the Rosenbergs. "You can explain to the Rosenbergs why you've been staying in their house," he said. He had never smiled more cockily. He gave the boys a broad wink, then he tapped the accelerator and drove sedately down Hillcrest, on his way out of Beverly Hills.

Taggart and Rosewood turned and saw Mr.

Rosenberg making for them. For a split second, Billie thought it *just* might be easier to shoot himself than to explain all this to the irate millionaire.

Maybe, he thought, *having Axel around wasn't quite as much fun as it had been a minute ago.*